The Eyes of a Man

Dawn Roberts

~~..~~

PUBLISH AMERICA

PublishAmerica
Baltimore

ISBN: 1-4241-7130-X
PUBLISHED BY PUBLISHAMERICA, LLLP
www.publishamerica.com
Baltimore

Printed in the United States of America

Dedicated to HG.

I'd like to thank all of the people who have shown me unwavering support throughout my writing career. Your guidance, input, and encouragement are the reasons this story is now in print. My heartfelt gratitude goes out to Deborah Styne, Vicki Hopkins, Jon, Alex, and Alyssa.

A special Thank You also goes to Debbe, Kim, Teg, Sarah, Amy, and Jill. Your excitement kept me going.

To all of you out there who have challenged a disability, diagnosis, or label in your lifetime…you are my inspiration!

Life is good!

Autumn

~~..~~

Chapter One

~~..~~

Alone in the corner, Mara Bartlett allowed her eyes to scan the crowd from her vantage point. For the pretty young woman, who generally had an easy smile for anyone, the frown on her face was an uncommon sight to behold. It was in no way related to the pink satin horror that Mara had been forced to wear, or the fact that her long brunette locks had been piled on top of her head in an unnatural up-do. These were both minor sacrifices that one expected for the privilege of being allowed to participate in a wedding.

She had been asked to be the maid of honor for her younger sister, and although not the cause of her present bleak mood, the man asked to stand up as the best man was.

It was all too cliche, Mara thought to herself—the age-old story—the maid of honor detests the best man. In romance books, the two always found a way to fall in love, despite their turbulent beginning, but Mara held no illusion of that particular storyline playing out in their case. The man might be tall, dark, and something akin to decent looking, but on character alone, she formed a poor opinion of him.

Mara permitted dislike of the man to taint her pleasure in what should have been a joyous occasion, and selfishly she allowed herself to brood on it as her vision fell to the best man as he danced with the groom's sister with a sullen expression on his face.

Why was she not surprised that he looked miserable? Mara always thought he looked like he had a frown perpetually on his face.

At the rehearsal the night before, this man, William Grant, had displayed a level of anal retentiveness she had never witnessed in another person, convincing Mara that his perverse need for order was a sign of an individual in need of psychiatric help.

Everything had to be planned to accommodate his suggestions and desires, every single move. William had single-handedly sucked dry all the festive atmosphere from the evening, and the rehearsal practice that should have lasted an hour, took three.

William had wanted to know exactly how many steps there were from the altar to the back of the church. He walked it twice to count them himself. When was his cue to turn around? How close did he and Mara follow the bride and groom? Could the candelabra be moved to a place behind him? These were but a sampling of the endless questions he had asked.

Mara could have overlooked the annoyance she felt as simply his nerves getting the better of him had William not verbally insulted her when she was but five feet away from him. While the bride's attendants were readying to leave for the rehearsal dinner, William took the groom-to-be aside and spoke in hushed tones. She overheard William request, "Please don't ask me to dance with Jane's sister tomorrow, especially after the pictures are taken."

Greg told him that it was out of the question, but William held firm, confessing that no argument would sway his resolve not to dance. Mara's first reaction was a string of cussing so biting it could not be uttered, not even in the privacy of her own mind. Fortunately, she had the self-control not to say the words aloud.

Even the most confident person would have been hard-pressed not to feel the sting of William's slight. It was embarrassing to be considered so unworthy and unattractive that a dance would be a punishment, regardless that their pairing was a part of the traditional first dance of the newly married couple.

Apparently, the groom's sister was a much more suitable dance partner, but then she was part of the wealthy New York contingent that had been invited to the reception. Mara stood in judgment of the two men who were still conversing in hushed voices, and acknowledged that her sister had done a good job in her choice of a husband, despite his deplorable city friend.

The groom, Greg Masters, was from New York money. A third-generation chain drugstore heir, he bought a stately country property in Vermont to escape the pressure of big city living. Not a month after he had moved to the area, Greg developed an allergy he just couldn't shake. Mara's sister, Jane, worked as a nurse in town, and she was the one who took care of Greg when he came into the doctor's office for his allergy shots. Soon, they became inseparable.

After dating for three months, Jane moved in with Greg, and that was when Mara found out there was more to her sister's suitor than she had been led to believe. Greg was also known in certain circles as Christian Moore, the author of the mainstream *Lore Keeper* series of vampire books.

William Grant was Greg's closest friend, and it was apparent to Mara that inherited wealth was a common denominator between the two men. Whereas Greg was openly friendly to everyone he came into contact with, William reeked of pretentiousness from the advantages he had been given. He and the other New Yorkers appeared disillusioned by the groom's choice in a wife, and the division between those who worked for their money and those who were born lucky became clear as the wedding neared.

Mara condemned William because he represented all the super rich, self-important people she'd ever encountered. His demanding nature, his rudeness, and his conceit were simply other reasons for her to avoid the man. The rehearsal was not their first meeting but their third, and the other two had not gone well, either.

She had noted William's tendency to stare at her at the most inopportune times, as if he didn't even care if he were caught in the act, and she was certain that he was searching for some defect in her. Mara's assumption was confirmed when she recalled the time she had entered a room he was occupying, and he blatantly ignored her presence the entire time she was there.

These memories only served to annoy Mara, and she wondered why she'd spent any amount of time during her sister's wedding day to ponder them. It took a moment more before Mara realized that the song had ended, and the bride was preparing to toss her bouquet. Back in the present, Mara's eyes were still focused on William as he stood out on the dance floor.

He was looking right back at her.

Two days after the wedding, the newlyweds were still at their home entertaining the guests they had staying with them. Soon they would be traveling to Mexico for their honeymoon, but as Jane reminded Mara when she told Jane that she should boot her guests out the door, she and Greg had been living together over a year. Jane claimed that having people with them after the wedding was not an inconvenience. One of those who stayed was William Grant.

Mara had been invited to dinner with the few stragglers still in residence. What she didn't know was that earlier in the morning, an impromptu decision had been made by the remainder of Greg's family to head back to New York a day early, which left only the happy couple, William, and Mara at the table.

When she entered the Masters' home, the domestic scene Mara walked into was one she would never have expected to find, at least not from two men who led privileged lives—William and Greg were cooking, while Jane sat idle at the kitchen island sipping a glass of wine.

As the daughter of a fourth-generation farmer, it was understandable that she was fairly intimidated by the obvious wealth that surrounded Greg and William. It made her feel as if she had to compensate for her own family's very average lifestyle, and though Greg had never once made an issue of her family's few assets, she still felt the need to keep that defense mechanism firmly in place within her.

Just as she was about to announce her arrival, William laughed at a comment Greg made to him. His laughter was a sound Mara had not heard in the past, and from what she could tell there was light banter going on between the friends—it all sounded so *normal*. In the brief span of time before she was detected, Mara felt as if she were watching the two of them as they naturally were with each other, when the eyes of others were not upon them.

From the moment Jane noticed her and told her to come and join them, William gave Mara no reason to find fault with him. He spoke directly to her, welcoming Mara by telling her it was good to see her again, and then falling into a quieter mood than the one she had observed just minutes before. It was the first time Mara had seen William so at ease, and it surprised her.

Dinner was not an uncomfortable situation due in part to the fact that Mara was determined to set aside her personal resentment of William for the duration of the meal. Greg and Jane carried most of conversation, but Mara kept turning back to the topic of his books. She thoroughly enjoyed needling Greg for information about what direction his characters were going to take next, even though she knew that her brother-in-law generally remained tight-lipped about his stories.

Pointing her finger at Greg, Mara's grin was genuine. "I'm still furious with you for making me have sympathy for Absit. I want to hate him, yet he's so damn despondent. Have Jane get him a prescription for an anti-depressant and tell him to snap out of it."

"I think he's more of a candidate for an anti-psychotic, myself," Jane laughed as she gave her opinion. "In just two more semesters, I'll be able to write him one myself."

"See, Greg! Jane's willing to do it!" The three of them continued on teasing each other until another voice entered the fray.

"I find it interesting that you have compassion for Absit." William directed his comment toward Mara, his tone considerate. He had been enjoying the camaraderie these three shared, and the good-natured joking encouraged him to join in.

Mara paused briefly before answering him. "It's hard not to mourn for Asbit. His back-story is revolting, but his state of mind is dismal, for lack of a better word. Yes, I do sympathize with him."

"You approve of how he's portrayed?" Once again there was earnestness in William seeking her opinion, yet it did nothing to diminish Mara's impression that she might be taking a risk by responding. She still didn't trust William not to try to use her words to judge her or turn them against her to ridicule her.

"I like Greg's writing. There hasn't been one character in his books that I haven't formed an affinity for, good or bad. And I'm not just saying that because he so wisely married my sister."

"I may need your help soon with the science angle I'm working on, but I'll wait to ask your opinion until after I have the plot all figured out," Greg interjected.

"I didn't know you were an expert in science, Mara. Is that the type of teacher you are?"

"I teach chemistry and biology at our public high school."

Mara waited for him to make a patronizing comment about her profession, or rattle off statistics about how American children's education lagged behind other industrialized countries. However, William's only response to her declaration was the small smile he gave before he returned to his previous somber silence.

Mara's expectation of being ridiculed was not based on experience, since William had never made a disparaging comment about her before, other than his request that he not be made to dance with her. That wound was still fresh because it played against her self-confidence, and although Mara was not a woman to hold a grudge for long, she did have a tendency to dwell on things that bothered her. That was why she had avoided him for the rest of the wedding reception, so at least she could say she never had to dance with William Grant. It comforted her injured pride a little.

She had not taken into account the possibility that William had a legitimate reason for making his request of Greg, or that there might be extenuating factors that guided him to do so. Mara didn't know him well enough to even guess at what might be the cause.

The friendliness that William showed her at tonight's dinner table didn't seem contrived, but Mara only had her past interactions with the man on which to base her decision about his sincerity, and he didn't have a very good track record. Noting that he was once again staring at her, and experiencing the same uncomfortable feeling that it always gave her, Mara dropped her gaze to her plate, hoping that William would take the hint and stop looking at her.

"Mara was going to be a pharmacist, you know," Greg enlightened his friend. "She's really quite knowledgeable about medicine. Reads everything she can get her hands on."

William made no comment as his brow furrowed, but his eyes never faltered from the woman across from him.

"You would say that, Greg," Mara responded dryly. "That was a few years ago."

She knew that Greg was proud that she had been accepted into the highly competitive college of pharmacology, but it remained a subject not often discussed within Mara's family. Being accepted had been the highlight of her life, an accomplishment for which she had worked hard, and when she had to abandon the dream, it was more devastating than Mara ever admitted.

Peering over at Jane, Mara was curious if she could see any reaction from her sister about her decision not to pursue her degree. There was none. Jane appeared as she always had—confident and oblivious to the sacrifice Mara had made for her.

Not in the three years since Mara had been faced with the dilemma of leaving college, had she and Jane talked about it, and it was doubtful they ever would. Jane had continued in college toward her own advanced degree, which would soon earn her a nurse practitioner license.

By the end of dinner, Mara had finished three glasses of wine which meant two things—her tongue was looser, and she was going to stay in her sister's guestroom instead of driving home. It was late when they all went to their respective beds, but on a whim, Mara decided to stay up to enjoy what was left of the fire that had been burning in the grate.

Some time after midnight, her solitude was broken when she heard someone coming down the hallway. She prayed it wasn't William, but it was a prayer not to be answered. Once he entered the living room, Mara turned on a light to let him know it was occupied, in hopes he would return to his room.

"I don't need the light," William stated as he raised a hand to shield his eyes. He stood still while he waited for her to turn it back off. Like Mara, he was seeking out the last remnants of the fire, but unlike her, he had hoped she would still be awake.

William turned his head to look around before posing a question. "Will you tell me where the chair is?"

"About three steps to your left."

Mara watched William follow her instructions before sitting down. She had not thought the light was that intense, yet she felt she needed to say words of apology since she had evidently caused the man discomfort.

"I'm sorry for blinding you."

"Think nothing of it."

Many minutes passed where the only sound in the room was the ticking of the clock. Mara had almost forgotten William was there as she slipped nearer sleep, until he spoke to her in a tone barely above a whisper.

"Why didn't you become a pharmacist?"

Perhaps it was because she was drowsy, but Mara didn't have the energy to take offense with a virtual stranger asking such a personal question of her.

"My father was diagnosed with cancer while Jane and I were in college. She was a year away from getting her bachelors degree. I still had two years of the masters program left. One of us had to drop out to help him."

"Is there a reason why you haven't returned?"

"You'd never understand," she answered gently. William received no more clarification as more minutes ticked by.

"I want to ask you a question." It was Mara's turn to break the silence.

"Please do."

"Why do you keep staring at me? What have I done? What are you looking for?"

"It's a habit, and I meant no disrespect by it. I didn't realize…" William stumbled over his explanation. If Mara had opened her eyes, she would have perceived sincere remorse in his expression.

"It's very unnerving, William, and it leads me to believe you're searching for the flaws I admittedly have." Although her words were to the point, they were not delivered with brusqueness. William's rebuttal was immediate.

"I apologize if I gave you that impression. It was unintentional."

"Thank you for explaining. I have to say that's a bit of a relief."

Over the stereo a song with a commanding beginning played while Mara shifted her position to get more comfortable, but soon the music mellowed and tranquility in the room was reestablished.

"Mara, are you still here?"

"I'm in the chair across from you. Don't you see me?"

Shaking his head, William answered. "No."

His disclosure stole the drowsiness away from Mara, and she sat up and leaned toward him. Between the illumination from the fireplace and the numerous nightlights Jane and Greg had scattered throughout the house, she could easily make out William, down to the brown of his eyes. How he did not see her, Mara could not fathom, but the idea of it frightened her. She left her seat on the couch and walked across the room to kneel in front of William.

"Is something wrong? Do you want me to get Jane?"

"There's no need." William turned toward the sound of her voice, aware of the anxiety in it. "Didn't they tell you?"

"Tell me what?"

Feeling Mara take his hands into her own, William could sense her concern, and what should have been a very easy question for him to answer suddenly became difficult. Hesitating, William was tempted to give her the textbook definition he delivered whenever he came across a person who was not aware of the condition he lived with. It was dry and impersonal, purposely worded so that they might not seek clarification from him. It was, in a sense, William's defense.

Drawing breath, he opted for a simpler explanation so that if Mara wished to know more, he could tell her in his own words.

"I have a sight impairment."

"Sight impairment? Do you mean like night blindness?"

"Yes," William admitted, "but it's more complex than that. I have trouble with bright light, too."

A cascade of awareness hit Mara at that moment, as did emotions she was unprepared for—from fury at Jane and Greg for not letting her know William had difficulty seeing, to extreme disappointment in herself. Her face showed it all as accountability for her own actions set in, but William did not witness it.

Mara's initial impression of William had all the characteristics of a misunderstanding, based on conjecture and lack of facts. Had she known, Mara never would have allowed herself to judge him as she had.

"—That's why I stare—to focus, but I agree with you that I need to check myself. I wouldn't want someone gawking at me."

The horror Mara experienced when William made reference to her remark was wholly unplanned on his part. He had just wanted to make her more at ease, but it backfired.

"I'm so sorry I said that to you."

"Please, don't."

Sympathy was not what William wanted to hear from Mara. He had grown tired of people approaching him differently once they became aware of his blindness, and quite frankly, William was glad for her counsel. Few others would have mentioned it to him.

"Mara, it's not your fault. Bad genes are the cause."

There was a long, uncomfortable silence before Mara felt able to speak. She was ashamed of herself, which was a natural reaction to have, but she also required a moment to absorb what William had told her, as she began to think about his past actions in a different light.

It made sense now, and Mara understood why he had been so particular about his movements in the church. As she allowed herself to replay other situations where she had censured William for what she had considered arrogant conduct, including the occasion when he didn't acknowledge her presence when she had entered the room, the more pronounced her mortification became.

It didn't matter to Mara that she never openly told William off for his behavior in the past until tonight. Her very thoughts were viewed as deeds in her mind, and Mara needed him to forgive her, even if William would never be told the specifics of her sins.

"I'm sorry," she began, searching for the words that could best describe her regret.

"You don't need to—."

"Yes I do, for myself. Will you please let me tell you that I'm sorry and not take it away?"

"Okay." William smiled, letting Mara have her say.

"I'm sorry, William."

"Apology accepted, although—."

"William!" Mara knew William was teasing her so that she wouldn't take her error too seriously, and she felt a lessening in the tenseness within her. It was appreciated, though undeserved, and any remorse she felt would be short lived if he had his way in the matter.

Still holding William's hands in her own, Mara looked into the eyes of a man who could not clearly see her, and she wondered what sort of person he was like when not cloaked in the flaws she had placed upon him since the day they had been introduced.

She didn't know, and Mara had to have trust that William was not the man she had invented in her imagination. In her first act of faith based on her now clearer insight, Mara answered the question he had posed to her before the disclosure of his condition came to light.

"I didn't pursue pharmacology because I was a solid B student from a middle class family. There were no substantial scholarships that I could receive, and student loans wouldn't cover my tuition. My father had medical insurance when he was diagnosed with prostate cancer, but he was still left with a mountain of bills."

Nodding his head, William waited for her to continue.

"Two daughters in college was too much for my father to take on financially, and either Jane or I needed to drop out."

"You didn't believe I would understand that?" he asked, curious as to how Mara would have formed that impression.

"Has lack of money ever kept you from what you've wanted to do?"

"No," William responded honestly, "but it hasn't bought me everything I've wanted, either."

The following morning after Greg left to take William to the train station, Mara joined her sister in her bedroom as Jane packed for her honeymoon. Neither she nor William had confronted the couple in regard to not informing her about William's sight deficiency. Each had their reasons for remaining silent, but as Mara listened to Jane describe how wonderful her life was while placing her negligees in a suitcase, Mara's disappointment in her own sister began to come forth.

"William has retinitis pigmentosa," Mara stated calmly when there was a lull in her sister's narration.

"Yes."

"Why didn't you tell me?"

"You didn't know?" From the look in her eyes, it was clear Jane truly had no idea that Mara had been unaware of his situation.

"Not until last night when *William* enlightened me."

"I'm sorry. I thought Greg had said something to you. William is his friend, after all."

Not willing to allow Jane to pass the entirety of the blame off onto her husband, Mara pressed the issue. It was not her design to make Jane feel guilty over her misstep in judgment, but rather that she wanted her to understand the importance of her omission. If Mara had known beforehand, she would have taken steps to ensure William would have had any aid he might have required at the wedding, instead of leaving him on his own.

"You probably should have mentioned it to me, Jane. You're my sister."

"I had a lot on my mind." Jane then proceeded to list for Mara the burdens and aggravations she had suffered lately. It was in sharp contrast to the wonderful life she had been describing before Mara had confronted her. "Look, going to graduate school, working, and getting married was a little too much at once. But don't act like I didn't tell you about William on purpose."

"I didn't say you did it on purpose—" Left unsaid were the numerous opportunities before the wedding when Jane had not told Mara. Her lack of action was inconsiderate by Mara's standards, especially toward William.

She didn't want to argue with Jane, and quite frankly, Mara realized that she would not be able to win. Jane didn't often admit to being wrong, but in the past had shown that she rarely made the same mistake twice.

"We worked everything out ourselves," Mara conceded, believing that her point had been made.

"Was William angry?"

"No. He was very nice about it."

I'm sorry," Jane admitted sheepishly, after she had thought for a while. "I get too caught up in myself sometimes."

Reaching out, Mara touched her sister's arm to let her know there were no hard feelings. Jane was not a wholly selfish woman, but she did occasionally lose sight of others when she was preoccupied with what she wanted to achieve in her own life. It was simply a part of who Jane was, and those that loved her had learned to accept it.

Walking out to her car as she departed for home, Mara was greeted by the scent of autumn as it hung heavy in the air. The soil continued to retain the warmth summer left behind, but the brightly colored leaves that had just begun to fall from their branches reminded her that change was indeed in motion.

Opening his wallet, William felt the bills for one that was folded on the upper left hand corner marking it as a twenty. He did this as a secondary measure in case he wasn't able to make out the numbers on the money. Sometimes he could, but other times he could not, and it was better to be safe then to tip more than the cab fare.

Going up the steps to the brownstone he owned, William unlocked the door as the welcome relief of familiarity overcame him. Stepping over the area where he knew the mail would be lying on the floor from the slot in the door, he then closed and locked the door behind him. Everything had its place in his home, surprises being nonexistent unless someone was staying with him.

He had a very good time at Greg's wedding, and though William regretted not being more outgoing while he had been there, he thought he handled himself well, considering all the new situations he had been thrown into.

The lighting in the church had been terrible and was the single most difficult obstacle William had to contend with during the service. The sun coming through the stained glass windows had created shadows within the sanctuary that played tricks on his eyes, but with practice, he was able to differentiate what was real and imaginary. This made it possible for him to walk the aisle without drawing attention away from the bride and groom.

William was also glad he had seen Mara again, and that he had actually been able to talk to her alone for once. The fact that she not being informed about his condition could have been awkward for them both, but once it was explained, they fell into easy conversation with each other.

If she had lived in Manhattan, William would have asked her out for a date that very night, and that would have been no small feat for a man who rarely dated. Besides her physical beauty, there were elements of Mara's personality that William found attractive. What they were, he could not exactly pinpoint, but William was certain that her appeal wasn't only physical.

She also brought out in him a bashfulness he had not experienced since his younger days. It made no sense for him to feel like a schoolboy when Mara was near, but in spite of his best efforts to put his best foot forward, William knew that was how he acted around her—tongue tied and uncertain of himself.

William hoped she was able to see past the nervousness he had difficulty controlling, but what would it accomplish if she could? Mara had her life in Vermont, and he lived in Manhattan. The logistics of the distance between them were enough to discourage him from formally making his interest known—that and his belief that a woman like Mara surely did not want for male attention.

Last night William had spent time with the most impressive, real woman he had been introduced to in a long time. Besides being vibrant and warm, she had a direct and honest manner about her that came through when she spoke.

Mara had laughed at him when he was funny and disagreed when she felt she was right. It was almost two in the morning when she had peacefully fallen asleep next to him on the couch, with her head tilted toward him. William's eyes had fully adjusted to the lighting in the room by then, and he was able to watch her for a while before he determined that it was wrong for him to do so, remembering she had said it was an unnerving trait he possessed.

She was about as far removed from some of the women in William's social set as one could be. Women like Greg's sister, Carrie, whose greatest accomplishment many days was successfully shopping for new shoes. He had no patience for the idleness most of his friends surrounded themselves with—parties and gossip being the core of their existence. William readily recognized the only appeal he held for some of his former girlfriends had been his bank account.

His sight might have been hindered by his condition, but his other senses had been sharpened to accommodate the deficit. What people didn't realize was that William could hear the sincerity in their tone. He could tell when someone was only pretending to be interested in him, and he knew how to protect himself.

If the truth be told, many of the women he had dated were no more interested in William than he was in them. When he would enter a room, it was not uncommon for William to become instantly fascinating to those women who were seeking a properly connected and wealthy husband, but realistically, he knew he was not a prime first choice.

Women were not the only ones to play the game. William had male acquaintances who also displayed a tendency toward thoughtlessness. They would sleep their way through the masses of eligible society females, bragging about their conquests, and living only for the day that the ideal trophy wife was discovered.

His own parents had been of that mindset, and their example was one William swore he would never follow. His mother was beautiful and his father rich, and their union was based on little else. The relationship did not last long after he was born, according to the whispers from the people who knew them best, but they were able to maintain a convincing charade of contented matrimony for years afterwards.

Traveling the stairs that led to the second story, the echo of William's footsteps filled the void of the empty home. The brownstone was realistically too large for just one person, but with no siblings to share it and his parents no longer living, it was his alone.

Once his suitcase was deposited in his room, William sank into the chair at his desk in his home office and listened to the messages on his answering machine. It was comforting to be home, but there was a part of him that had remained in Vermont. His mind kept circling back to Mara, even when he told himself it was a fruitless venture. She had left an impression. Unfortunately, the more he thought about her, the more he realized how lonely he actually was.

Winter

~~..~~

Chapter Two

~~..~~

Mara had always cherished winter break from school, both as a student and now as a teacher. It was two weeks of heavenly freedom in which she wasn't accountable to the school administration, her students or their parents. She was her own person, and she could do as she pleased.

A self-reliant individual by nature, Mara didn't require a constant barrage of friends nearby to feel complete. The phone did seem to ring quite often, though, with calls from her sister and parents. More often than not, she turned down their offers to go shopping or out for a night on the town, as she settled in for a season of hibernation with a pile of good books and projects around her house that she had earmarked to do during the break.

Yet, as the days passed, the solitude she had once reserved for only winter was beginning to become more a part of her everyday life. There was a distance Mara kept from others that went unnoticed by most of her acquaintances, although she would readily break it when family obligations were at hand.

Until recently, no one had attempted to look below her surface to examine why Mara guarded herself as she did. This introversion had not always existed in her, and there was a time when she was the most outgoing of Thomas Bartlett's two daughters. The detachment began when she decided to come home from college to help her mother care for her father as he battled cancer, while taking what courses she could to complete her teaching degree.

One of her aunts once commented that Mara had matured during that period in her life, but it was really that she had withdrawn. Her father beat his cancer, the farm was maintained, and life slowly began to return to normal for the rest of the family. Still, no one questioned Mara in depth about herself during that time or in the years afterwards. Except William.

That night three months ago, after William had told her about his sight impairment, Mara realized that he was someone not terribly unlike herself. He was inquisitive, and Mara answered many of his questions, even though the almost shy way in which William induced her to open up had made her uneasy at first. Mara wasn't one to discuss her private thoughts, but that evening she had stayed up until the wee hours in the morning doing exactly that.

She learned something important from their encounter. It was that William was human and he need not intimidate her. With just one long conversation, Mara realized William wasn't the elitist snob she had branded him before she had taken the opportunity to get to know him. Granted, his opinions were influenced by his upbringing, but she couldn't detect that he thought less of people who did not share the same advantages he had.

She would have liked to have had the chance to know him better, if for no other reason than that he inadvertently encouraged her reevaluate her own bias. Mara had to admit that William was handsome, too, but that appeal was secondary to her logical mind.

William had only returned once to Vermont since Jane's wedding while Mara was away at a teaching seminar, but otherwise, the opportunity for their paths to cross was nonexistent. Mara didn't often allow her thoughts to dwell on him, as she had convinced herself there was nothing really to think about. William was a good man who she might encounter every once in a while, and that was it, she told herself.

Regardless of how much she wanted to believe her denial of any true interest in William, on the few occasions that she had been to her sister's home since the wedding, Mara waited with anticipation for them to mention him, which Greg always did. She tucked away the bits of information given to her without comment and added the knowledge to the details that she already knew of the man.

The ringing of her telephone woke Mara from her sleep on a chilly January morning. On the line was an irritated Jane, who was supposed to be on her way to a medical conference. The snow had fallen heavily the night before, closing school for the day, and unbeknownst to Mara who was still warm in bed, flurries had restarted that morning.

Jane had foolishly tried to make it to her destination two hours from her home. She was stranded on the side of the highway due to a spin-out on an icy patch on the roadway. After explaining she was fine and that her car was merely stuck and not completely wrecked, Jane made a request of her sister.

"Greg is coming to get me. Would you please do me a favor and go over to the house and stay by the phone for a while in case we have trouble getting back? The radio said they were considering closing the highway if the snow continues, and I'm worried about William being there alone all day."

"William's at your house?"

"He has been for the past two days."

"No one said anything to me." There was a slight bite to Mara's statement. Jane was not obligated to inform her when she and Greg had company, but she thought it would have been noteworthy enough to be mentioned in passing.

"I'm sure I did, because I was wondering why you hadn't stopped by."

"No, Jane. I'm starting to believe that if I don't fax you, you don't pay attention." Jane made no response to her sister's comment because it was true. "I'll drive over after I shower to see about William. My cell phone will be with me."

Getting out of bed, Mara went to her bedroom window and looked outside. The snow had blanketed the countryside, covering the dead of winter with unsoiled splendor. From a distance, she could see her uncle's dogs running through the white powder, the exuberance in their stride unprecedented for the aging animals. They moved across the bare field as if they were dancing, as the snow had undoubtedly aroused the youthful spirit they once had.

It was mesmerizing, and Mara could have easily lost track of time while standing there as the flakes fell silently from the sky. The wind abated, and if she was going to drive over to Jane's house, Mara realized that now was the time to leave. With no one else around to witness, she grinned restlessly to herself as she allowed the curtains to fall back over the window.

The idea of seeing William again, after so much time had passed, summoned feelings of both anticipation and foreboding inside of her. Was he really as attractive as she thought, or had she built him up so much in her mind that he could never live up to the illusion into which she had fashioned him? Mara didn't have an answer for herself.

She believed that William's life in New York was undoubtedly full—the urban environment was so foreign to her that it was as if she only had books and movies to tell her what it must be like. Mara had been to the city enough that she was not in awe of it, but she had not spent any real time with a person who actually resided there.

Not allowing herself to linger too long on her provincial deficiencies, or exalt the sophistication of those who existed amongst the multitude, Mara brought a pair of jeans and a sweater out of her closet and set out for the shower.

Less than an hour later, she was calling out William's name after entering through the side door of her sister's home. The onset of a blizzard was blowing outside, and legitimate concern for Jane's well-being weighed heavy on Mara as she hung up her coat.

William answered from the same room Mara had found him in the last time they had met, and awkward greetings were exchanged in the kitchen. A period of silence ensued in which both appeared embarrassed and somewhat unsure about what to say next, as they secretly worried that the other could read their minds and know what they had been thinking.

Mara was not alone in her desire to be reacquainted. Since he had arrived in Vermont, William had questioned Greg more than once about her, and was going to suggest that Greg invite her over that evening for dinner, but that would now be unnecessary. The impression Mara had made on him was one William could not quite let go of, and he was very glad to see her again. Unfortunately the tongue-tied reaction he had to overcome the last time he had been in Mara's presence returned.

In an effort to squelch the self-conscious silence that had overtaken them, Mara told him of the situation involving Jane, but William was already aware of it. The reciting of facts was a wise move on her part, and it made it easier for them to keep the conversation going.

"Greg's going to call as soon as he reaches her," William shared as he removed the pan he was making breakfast in from the heat. "From what he said ten minutes ago, a tow truck was on its way, and the highway is being closed."

"Do you know if they're going to take the back routes home?"

"He didn't say, but he thinks they may have to get a hotel until the road is reopened."

"You might be stuck with me for a while." Mara sighed as she laid her phone on the table.

"You don't have to stay unless you want to. I don't want you to feel obligated to wait the storm out with me. I'm resourceful and can handle myself if you leave."

Realizing that he had just said the same thing three different ways, and very quickly at that, William closed his mouth, vowing not to speak again until he could do so without making a fool of himself. If ever a man felt like he was reliving his clumsy adolescence years, it was William at this moment.

"But I'm not. My car barely made it here, because I kept getting caught in other people's ruts," Mara laughed before a random thought crossed her mind.

"Do you want me to leave, William?"

"No." William answered while tapping the spatula against the side of the pan.

Turning away from the stove, William shot Mara a quick glance, and then another so he could determine where she was standing. This action was not lost on her.

"You can look at me and I promise not give you a long-winded lecture again."

Grinning, William could hear the humor in Mara's voice.

"—That is," she added a stipulation. "As long as you share whatever smells so good coming from the stove."

"That would be our breakfast. When they told me you were coming, I went ahead and cooked for both of us."

"You're a godsend!"

It was as easy as that for Mara to become relaxed in his presence, and after a short time, William was relaxed in hers, too. Few people would have imagined that he would have been the more reserved of the two, most notably since William worked as a fundraiser and dealt with the public on a continual basis, but with Mara, he was reticent and there seemed to be no way to shake it.

"What are you making?" Peering around William, she stretched to see what was on the stove. Her belly was already responding to the aroma that occupied the kitchen.

"Omelets. Are you hungry?"

"Yes!" Walking over to the silverware drawer, Mara brought out forks and napkins for them and set the table. "I'm amazed that you cook. I assumed you had someone who did that for you."

"Why is that?"

"I don't know. My aunt cooks for my bachelor cousin all of the time. That boy can't open a cereal box without his mama's help. I guess I thought that was the norm."

"In New York, I do have someone who makes dinner for me, sometimes."

"A girlfriend?"

"No," Shaking his head, William reached for plates. "I pay someone to come in to straighten up and run errands. Wait, that sounds too impersonal. She's worked for my family since I was a little kid. Her name is Gladys, and she makes the best spaghetti I've ever tasted."

Listening to William share a glimpse of his daily routine, Mara admitted to herself how pleased she was that he told her there wasn't a girlfriend in the picture. Not that Mara had any illusion of her ever becoming so, but it made it so she could spend time with William without any of the guilt associated with cozying up to another woman's man.

"Is that where you learned to cook from?"

"Yes, actually, it is." William asked as he placed their breakfast on the table. "Do you like to cook?"

"I'm really appalling and prefer not to. And before you ask, I'm not being humble. I burn everything, so it all tastes the same to me."

"Burnt?" With his eyes full of mischief, William grinned at his own joke as he took a seat next to Mara.

"Very funny, and thank you."

"You're welcome."

Sitting side by side while they ate, they made idle small talk about the weather and such while shy smiles and stolen glances passed between them. Neither acted in a flirtatious manner during this time, it was more that they were both experiencing the stirrings of attraction, and their wanting to look at each other was a natural consequence of it.

"Tell me, what are you going to do today?" Mara asked as she poured more orange juice for herself and William.

"I was looking over Greg's story with him before your sister called. I don't know now."

"He lets you read it?" William didn't reply, but the incriminating expression on his face was enough for Mara to begin her interrogation. "Does he ever listen to you if you make a suggestion?"

"What is it you want me to tell him?"

"I'm so glad you asked." Pulling her chair closer to his, Mara moved her plate over and began giving William her wish list to mention to Greg. Before long, their communion turned effortless as subjects flowed freely and without the need of forethought.

* * *

Three hours later, they were laughing in the living room, sitting close to each other on the couch. Jane and Greg were safely deposited at a hotel and wouldn't return all day. As ungracious as it might seem, they weren't missed as much as they should have been, as William and Mara were doing quite well on their own.

With her body sideways and legs crossed, Mara recounted for William the hazards of being a teacher when the time came for the real science of biology to be explored.

"—So she comes in to the classroom on a Monday with a note from her mother about how she could not, in good conscience, dissect a frog. 'Passive observer' was the term I believe. This occurred *after* I saw the girl at Johnny's Restaurant when they were serving all-you-can-eat frog legs! William, I watched the child eat them."

"What did you do?"

"I marched down to the principal's office and explained the situation, then I called the mother and asked why her daughter could eat a frog, but not dissect one. I was convincing, too. The turning point might have been when I mentioned that for next year's class I was thinking about dissecting snakes, and did she think that when her daughter repeated my class, she'd prefer those?"

"You said that?" Mara proudly admitted to William that she had. "You're a devil of a teacher."

"I take that as a compliment. The only one I let off the hook was the vegan girl who believes in a Buddhist version of reincarnation. Her story I believed. If the kids truly have an issue, I don't mind finding them something else to do, but the excuse has to be legitimate."

"You like teaching, don't you?" Leaning back against the couch, William relaxed with the smile he had worn most of the day.

"I think so, but I have to tell you a secret about the profession. You get paid in car wash tokens and free government cheese. I wish they would have told me that before I took the job!"

His laughter excited her own, and the harmony produced by the friendly conversation made time feel like it was flying. William couldn't remember the last time he had enjoyed himself as much while doing nothing but talking, and Mara was relaxed and completely herself.

No longer were the glances stolen that they shared, as William and Mara had no difficulty being genuine in showing their regard. There was *something* there between them that they both felt, and they were secure enough with the other person not to suppress it.

Once their mirth died down, she broached a subject she had wanted to ask William about for a while. Mara almost let it pass, since it was not of much importance anymore, but her curiosity got the best of her, and she decided to satisfy it.

"Why didn't you dance with me at the wedding, William? I think I know the reason, but I'd like to hear it from you."

"I didn't want to embarrass you or myself." He admitted honestly.

"That's not possible." Without thinking, Mara clasped her hands together around William's forearm.

"Trust me, it is."

"You danced with Greg's sister," Mara reminded William, her eyebrows arched in mock challenge.

"She's known me for years, and it was hours after the pictures were taken."

"Did the camera flash bother you?"

"Some." Shrugging, William left his explanation vague so that he wouldn't excite any sympathy. "I wanted to ask you to dance, but that doesn't count, does it? I am sorry for that."

"I wasn't searching for an apology," Mara reassured him, "but no, that doesn't count."

"Were you angry with me?"

"I don't know if angry is the right word. I think it's more accurate to say that I let my feelings get hurt."

"I *really* am sorry, Mara."

"Don't be sorry. I didn't know you then." Leaner a little closer toward him, Mara asked another question. "William, how much can you see?"

"The last time I was tested it was just under twenty percent of normal vision."

"You don't use a cane."

"No, not unless I have to."

"Do you have good days and bad days?"

Nodding his reply, William did not divulge to Mara that his pride was also a deciding factor. He was not ashamed of the cane, but for him it represented a reminder that there could come a time when he would no longer have a choice other than to be dependent on it, and he refused to use one until it became absolutely necessary.

Every time William had to adjust his life as a result of his vision decreasing, to him it was like taking a step toward the inevitable. There was nothing he or his doctors could do to stop the progression, so he made certain he remained as self-reliant as possible for as long as he could.

William's prognosis was not encouraging. His retinitis pigmentosa was diagnosed when he was in grade school. Constantly tripping and falling to a point where even strangers were beginning to make comments about it, his mother had taken him to the doctor expecting to be informed that her son had a balance problem, but that ended up not being the case. William's peripheral vision was the culprit.

His father also suffered from the same diagnosis, but the signs were so mild that it went unnoticed until after he learned of his son's condition. Because William had developed symptoms at a young age, his doctor warned his parents that it increased his chances that he would someday face the world without any vision at all. Every year brought him closer to fulfilling his doctor's prediction.

Mara gazed up at his face during the lull her question had created, and noticed an aspect about him that gave her pause. William had the most beautiful brown eyes she had ever seen. The irises had speckles of color in them—green and gold, and the dark lashes outlining them only drew attention to how perfect they were. In that moment, Mara could not fathom why God would have given him such beauty only to take away its usefulness.

* * *

Outside the snowfall lessened to a delicate flurry as the afternoon slipped away. The mood changed to somber while they made dinner together. This was when William told her the details about his parents dying in a car accident five years before. Mara did not have prior knowledge of the details, and she also did not read the society pages of the New York newspapers.

During William's turn to reveal himself, he faced the same wariness Mara had experienced the night he had asked why she never returned to college. A trait they shared in common was that, like Mara, William did not make it a habit to talk about his personal life. Practice and familiarity would be all they needed to bridge this gap, and it would come over time.

"I didn't know your mother and father passed away," Mara said as she put down the knife she was using to cut onions and took his hand. "How old were you when it happened?"

"Twenty three."

"That's too young to lose your parents."

"It is." He agreed as he turned back to what he was doing. Then William felt softness press against his cheek. It was a kiss from Mara.

"Will you tell me about them?"

William described in detail for her how his father had been a fundraiser for different organizations, and that he followed in his father's footsteps instead of continuing on to study law. The fondness in which William spoke about his father was obvious. Mara thought there must have been a great deal of love between them because William spent the bulk of his description on his father's personality instead of his accomplishments.

"He could be a very funny man when the mood hit him."

"What about your mother? What was she like?"

"She was a handsome woman. She still has a sister living in New York."

"Did she have a sense of humor like your father?"

"No, I can't say she did." This was all William said about his mother, but it was enough for Mara to understand that his memories of her were not as pleasant as those he had of his father.

While dinner was cooking, Mara went over to the window to see if the snowfall had ended.

"It's over, William."

"That's good." He replied without much enthusiasm. William and Mara realized that once the storm passed, they weren't going to have the same unique opportunity with each other again. They had already heard on the radio that Mara's school had been called off for the next day, and they still had the rest of the evening together. But there was an element of romance to the way the snowfall had kept others at bay while they had a chance to get to know each other, and once it ended, it was if time was running out and reality would soon return.

Greg and Jane would return tomorrow, and William would leave for home in two more days. Looking over her shoulder to tell him what was occurring outside, Mara saw that William was staring at her, but it was not as she had observed in the past. He was not attempting to focus his eyes, she knew this because they weren't moving, and instead he was admiring her from a distance.

Mara was physically attracted to William, there was no need for her to deny it, and she hoped this was a sign that he also experienced it. She wouldn't have to wonder for long. Crossing the room to rejoin him at the counter, Mara stood next to him and William's arm went around her shoulder.

After dinner was over and the kitchen was clean, they returned to the living room with an identical secret inside of them—they had both found someone they wanted to spend more time with. Their differences only made them interesting to each other, and there was enough commonality between their minds that they had a solid foundation on which to build.

The sun had long past set, and just as they were about to enter the room, Mara turned and asked, "Will you tell me how to work the lights so they don't effect your sight?"

William stopped her in the hallway, reaching up to cup her chin in his hand. Her thoughtfulness prompted him to finally act on what he had wanted to do for hours, and that was to know what it was like to kiss her. The magnetism he felt for Mara was mightier than his modesty, and as his lips neared hers, William waited for a sign giving him permission. He received it, when Mara's arms wrapped around his neck and her lips covered his first.

William felt it when she kissed him, the sensation that courses through the body when two people connect with each other. Whether the impact is chemistry or emotion, it's not important because the physical proof is present, and it doesn't matter where it came from.

As his hands ran down her arms, William could feel the skin prickle underneath his palms. "You're cold," he whispered against her ear, remarking on the goosebumps he had touched.

"No, I'm not," she whispered back, and with those words, William knew Mara felt it, too.

Indulging in the silkiness of Mara's parted lips against his, William was the one to initiate a second kiss.

The next hour began innocently as they returned to their places near each other on the couch, then it turned passionate as inhibitions were lost somewhere between the words. Their advancement toward intimacy developed so naturally, that it didn't seem rushed to either of them.

They had been touching each other in places, in wonderful places that left them wanting more of each other. Mara was not the type of person to sleep around, but she had no hesitation about being with William this night. The fire building inside of her did not make that decision. It came from her heart. The progression was much the same for him. The longer William was with her, the more Mara was becoming his idea of the ideal woman. Imperfect, impassioned, forthright, and intelligent.

"William," Mara murmured nearly inaudibly as her body encircled his. William's hands were under her sweater against her bare back, and her lips were raw against his neck.

"Hmm?"

"I'm not an *easy* woman. It's important to me that you to know that. I never do this. I mean, I have, but not this soon."

"I didn't think you were." He answered seriously.

"Then you should also know that I don't want to stop."

Hearing Mara admit that she wanted him, coupled with the attraction he could literally feel coming from her, gave William a high he hadn't felt in years. Never in his wildest imagination would he have believed that this night would have taken the direction it was headed, as it was not something he had planned for or even thought about, and it was more right than anything he had done in a long time.

"Let's not stop." Opening his eyes, Mara was too close for William to see her, but when he brought one of his hands up to her cheek, he could feel her smiling. Then and there he decided that this was one woman he wasn't going to let slip through his fingers.

"I'm going to go look for something. I don't carry *that* around with me." Even after all she had just told William, Mara could not bring herself to say the word condom. "Do you have any?"

"No," he laughed gently.

"Will you meet me in your room?" The depth of his kiss told Mara he would.

It did not take long for Mara to return to William with a devilish grin he could see from the doorway. "I have a riddle for you. What do you get when you combine a drugstore family and a nurse?"

"I don't know. What?"

Mara dumped her find from Jane's medicine cabinet onto the bed. "A lot of free samples."

Looking down at the pile of condoms Mara had pilfered from his friends, the humor of their present situation was not lost on him. Here William was, under the influence of this pretty lady who was at that exact moment wiggling out of her jeans, and all he could think of to do was to confess their sins. "We are the worst houseguests ever!"

"Let's see." Mara teased as she pulled her sweater over her head. "We ate their food, drank their wine, and stole their condoms."

Crawling up on the bed, Mara scooped up the condoms and put them on the nightstand before she beamed him a huge smile. "Yep, I think you might be right."

William removed his own clothes while Mara pulled the bedspread back. Neither showed signs of having second thoughts about the love they were about to make. Once again, it simply felt right, as if the timing and every other element of their day had been perfectly arranged by a force greater than themselves. Instead of shyness, joy existed between them, and the laughter and smiles did not detract from the seriousness of what they were to share.

With his hand on the light switch, William caught one last glimpse of Mara in all her glory as she stretched out across the mattress, and the sight of her stopped him in his tracks.

"What's wrong?" She asked, suddenly concerned that her body might not be what he had expected. Tugging at the sheet, Mara held it against her chest as she waited for William to answer her.

"Damn."

"Good damn or bad damn?"

Shaking his head, William just couldn't stop grinning. "I can see you perfectly right now. Mara, it's a good damn."

"I like those the best." William took her outstretched hand before he turned out the light. Their skin was warm and the bed cool, but soon the sheets absorbed their heat as they took their time getting to know each other on an entirely new level.

"What are you doing?" Mara asked as she lie naked on her back while William's hands caressed her body with contact she could hardly detect. The evening was young enough that they needn't rush to the end.

"I'm looking at you." The room was dark except for a faint glow in the corner from a small light. "Close your eyes, and I'll show you."

"Okay."

"Your skin is smoother in this area. It must be where your waistband rubs against your skin. You have what I think is a mole right here." A circular motion was made on her breast where she did indeed have a small mole.

"Keep going," she sighed as the sensation of touch replaced that of sight.

"When my hand travels down," the pads of William's fingers ran slowly over her pelvis toward her thigh, "you catch your breath."

Reaching her hand out, Mara brought his head down to kiss her mouth. Mara's body was alive and receptive to every movement William made.

"You're so beautiful." She could feel William as his lips settled against her neck. Lowering his voice even more, he made a confession. "I thought so the first time I saw you. That's another reason I kept staring."

William's investigation continued as he grew aroused and Mara restless.

"I want to look at you now." Mara sat up and with the gentle prodding against his chest, William laid back. He asked her if her eyes were closed. They were. Mara then tried to imitate what he had been doing to her, although it was more difficult than she thought it would be.

Her eyes wanted to open, to visualize what it was she was admiring, but she continued in an attempt to break her habit of relying too much on what her mind told her she was seeing. She could feel muscle beneath the skin, and the broadness of William's chest. And when Mara held her hand to his sternum, the beating of his heart.

As she ran her lower lip over his, William pressed against her until she deepened the kiss. Passion grew, as movements quickened in anticipation, and the kiss deepened yet again. No explanation was necessary when Mara reached over to the nightstand to get a condom.

"You're incredible," Mara whispered as she straddled his torso and prepared him. In a long stroke she allowed William to enter her, enticing a low groan out of him as her body shivered when their hips met.

"How does that feel to you?" she asked breathlessly as she began the ancient movements of lovemaking. The rhythm Mara set was slow and deep, as she hoped to recreate the response of his initial entering her time and again.

"I can't describe it." William fought for the words as his mind clouded. How does one describe ecstasy? "It's intense. Carnal. I don't want you to stop moving until I can't take any more…but I want it to last for hours at the same time."

"I won't make it that long," Mara cried out against his shoulder as the overwhelming draw of lust now flowed through her veins, her mouth forming words William could not hear. It was a beautiful sight, right before Mara reached her peak, when she reopened her eyes wide and stared at William with wonder. Instinctively he pushed into her harder and this is what took her over the edge.

William could feel her tightening on him as she contracted, deep moans coming from her throat while sweat beads formed in the valley between her breasts. Hearing her pleasure made it impossible for him to contain his anymore, and with a warning that he couldn't wait, William released himself.

After they had taken a moment to cool down, William raked his fingers through her hair as she rose up to allow the heat between them to escape.

"How do you feel?" He asked tenderly.

"Like I don't want this to be a one night stand." Mara caught herself just as the final word came out, embarrassed at saying her thoughts aloud.

"I don't want it to be, either."

"William, you don't have to say that."

"Come closer." His arms reached out to pull her beside him, and she rested her head against his shoulder. He saw a beauty in her, one that did not require eyes to identify. "I'm serious."

It was far too soon for declarations of love to be shared, but not so for promises. William would come to Vermont on the weekends whenever he could, and he would call her often.

"—And after the snowplows have been out tomorrow, I'd like to take you out. Just you and me." Once William thought it would be impossible for him to have the chance to date Mara, but now that he had spent a day and night with her, he knew it was impossible for him not to be with her.

"We could go to the movies if they're open." William suggested, the genuineness of his offer causing her to smile down at him.

"Okay." Mara yielded, losing some of her embarrassment. "I could have you over for dinner, first."

With the taste of the burnt toasted cheese sandwich she made him for lunch revisiting his memory, William agreed, and their courtship officially began.

The clock on the nightstand glowed that it was three in the morning when Mara started whispering his name. His patience and her impatience had collided earlier and had created some of the most physical, yet tender intercourse she had ever had. They were lying face to face now, their bodies close and unclothed except for a blanket that covered them.

"William, are you awake?" Her breath was light against his shoulder.

"I can be." He nodded heavily on the pillow they were sharing.

"Will you look at me?"

"I probably can't see you very well, but I'll try." William opened his heavy lids making out a shadow of her form. The hues of gray and black in which he interpreted Mara still disclosed that she was a lovely woman.

"No," Mara took her hand and covered his eyes. "I didn't mean it like that. I meant *your* way."

The next afternoon William and Greg were sitting at his desk discussing the chapters Greg had recently completed. Mara had left late that morning before the couple had returned home to go help her father, leaving William alone to inform them about their plans for the night.

Both expressed approval over the match, as expected, and the subject was dropped once the details about time and place were given. That is, until Greg had William alone.

Despite his wife's subdued reaction, Greg was actually extremely happy for his friend. Until that day, he had never thought about suggesting Mara to William as a possibility, but once he heard that they had worked it out on their own, Greg wondered why he hadn't seen it coming.

Mara had just the right level of liveliness that he was convinced William needed in his life, and she was a woman he trusted not to have ulterior motives. He believed it to be a good match for her, too. Mara deserved a man who wouldn't play games with her and who would treat her with the respect she deserved.

"So, you're going out with Mara tonight?"

Rolling his eyes, William answered the same question for the fourth time. "Yes."

"She's very nice."

"I know."

"But a really bad cook."

"I know." William laughed as he pointed to his computer monitor to get Greg's mind back on what they were working on. He didn't mind talking about Mara, although he was grateful that the topic of the missing condom had not come up, but he and Greg only had today and tomorrow before William was to head back to New York.

They made good progress until Greg again raised the subject of another woman.

"How's your aunt doing?" Greg did not bother to disguise his contempt. "The one that hates me."

"You're in good company," William acknowledged. "I don't know. I went to her home on Christmas where she was holding court with her cronies. It was the same as it has been since my parents died. Catherine told me what I *should* be doing, and asked me if I was blind yet."

"What did you tell her?"

"I said not to worry about it. I'd still send her monthly checks, even if I couldn't see to sign them."

"Good for you."

"Catherine then gave me a watch and sent me away."

"She's a bitch." Greg knew he probably should have kept that opinion to himself, but he knew his friend wouldn't be offended by his admitting the truth.

"She's calmed down some in her old age."

Greg doubted William's claim. Catherine was too much like her sister, William's mother, and that woman didn't mellow with age.

Greg wanted to ask him why he didn't just financially cut off his aunt. William was under no obligations to follow through on the allowance his father had given to Catherine after her own husband had died, but he knew this was not open for discussion.

Changing the subject before he made a comment he might regret, Greg completed a full circle back to his sister-in-law.

"How are you going to work it out with Mara?" he grinned, fully aware that his pestering William about her was beginning to annoy him.

"I'll find a way. I think the train will be our friend."

"You can always stay here, when you want to come see her."

"I don't want to intrude too much."

"Don't let that stop you. Jane's gone all of the time."

Looking over at Greg, William was not certain whether he should let his friend's comment stand on its own, or if he should ask Greg what he meant by it. As recently as a month before their wedding, Greg had confided in him that they had been arguing about her never being around, but had worked it out.

One of the problems William saw was that Greg worked from home, and since he was there all of the time, Jane's absence was more noticeable to him. Jane had ambition, which Greg knew before he married her, but there was always that line between what one expects and what one receives.

Not feeling qualified to counsel his friend about matters in which he had little experience, William took a different approach.

"When does Jane receive her masters?"

"This is her last semester."

"Is she still working part time, too?"

"Yes. She wants to stay with that group of doctors once she's a nurse practitioner. Don't get me wrong. I'm not complaining, but thank God there is an end in sight. Besides, the area does need her."

"Things will slow down once Jane graduates." William was convinced of what he said. Greg and Jane were good people, and the optimist in him believed that any differences they had could be overcome.

"It will," Greg agreed.

"Does your father's company still offer scholarships?" An idea had come to William this morning, and now seemed like the time for him to approach Greg with it.

"Yes."

"Have you offered Mara one?"

"I did. She wouldn't take it."

In the hours they had spent talking the night before, this was a discussion William and Mara didn't have. Curious as to why she would have turned down what might have been an opportunity to finish her degree, William posed another question to Greg that he might not be able to answer.

"Mara doesn't want to go back to college?"

"No, that's not why she wouldn't take it. She said that her receiving it just because she knew me wouldn't be fair."

"So she didn't apply?"

"She did, but Mara didn't get it. She was in the final selection, though."

Chapter Three

~~..~~

Mara had been taught that she was always to call before she showed up at someone's house. Her mother had stressed this, as it was a personal irritation of hers when people arrived unannounced—always after her daughters had managed to make a mess or her husband had tracked mud through the kitchen.

So often did Mara's mother remind her children of her golden rule, that when Mara pulled up in Jane's driveway having totally ignored her wisdom, for a split second she felt a pang of guilt and thought about calling her sister. Then the guilt passed, as she realized that calling Jane from in front of her house asking permission to stop by was more overkill than politeness.

Her day had started out uneventfully. Mara had been sitting in her classroom while the students took their midterm exams, with no other occupation for her mind but to think about her upcoming trip to visit William. He had already been back to Vermont twice within a month, but this would be her first visit with him in New York. Though Mara wasn't nervous about seeing him again, she was beginning to have doubts about the plans he had made for their weekend.

In what best could be described as an extreme state of agitation, Mara left school as soon as the last bell sounded and drove straight to her sister's house. Luckily, Greg answered the door, letting her in without any questions and directing her to where his wife was studying.

"I need your help."

From a chair in her bedroom, Jane looked up from the textbook she had been reading. "What do you need?"

"Your full attention for ten minutes. Please, I'm serious. I need advice"

Nodding her head, Jane marked the page, before calmly placing the book on the floor. It took quite a bit to disturb the ever-composed Jane, and though Mara rarely came to her for advice, she was confident that they could tackle whatever problem was bothering her.

"What is it?"

"William's taking me out to a club on Saturday night." Casting Jane a withered expression, Mara believed those words would be all that was necessary to convey the dire predicament she was in. They weren't.

"What kind of club are you talking about?"

"A blues club, I think. Willow's Retreat?"

"Willow's Run." Jane smiled. "I've heard about it. You should have fun."

"And then he's inviting some friends of his so I can meet them."

"Who are they?"

"Christine and David Bass."

The names were unfamiliar to Jane, but that wasn't surprising considering she hadn't spent much time in New York getting to know Greg's friends. Nevertheless, Jane wanted to do something to help Mara because despite the unruffled demeanor she had whenever her sister would mention William to her, on the inside, Jane was very happy for Mara

"I don't know them. What is it that you need advice about?"

"Let's start with what I'm supposed to wear to go out. I really don't know what's expected of me. I don't want to show up looking like a hayseed."

Taken aback by her sister's disclosure, Jane hadn't considered that Mara would be anything but excited about her weekend with William, but then again, she never worried about fitting in to new situations. Jane simply adapted, without much planning or forethought.

"Hold on." Calling out for Greg to join them, Jane explained that he would have her answers. Mara would have chosen not to involve Greg in her dilemma, if she had a choice, but before she could relate this to Jane, he was in the room with them.

With a great deal of embarrassment, Mara turned to Greg and began her questioning.

"Will you tell me about Willow's Run?"

"I couldn't get reservations last time we were in town."

"More than that, Greg. What's it like?"

The description he gave was vague, but informative. The club had a reputation for drawing in talented musicians, often artists that were on the cusp of being discovered, and that was what made it so difficult to get in but worth the effort. It wasn't a place that people went to if they wanted to be seen, but there was a trendy undercurrent to being there.

"How do people dress when they go there?" This was the information Mara really needed. She knew she could handle herself socially without being a disgrace, but she didn't want to stand out from the crowd because she looked out of place.

"Um...I'd say dressy casual."

"Do you know David Bass?"

"I know of the family. William went to school with him."

"What are he and his wife like?"

"Nice."

"Greg, you say everyone's nice." Mara objected, holding her hands out in exasperation to stress her point. "But what are they *like*?"

"I don't say that everyone's nice."

"Yes, you do! I hear you say it all of the time."

"Not *everyone*." Greg denied, as if he was defending his own honor.

"I beg to differ..."

"There are a lot of people I don't like."

"Stop it, you two!" Jane interrupted. The sibling-like quality to Greg and Mara's argument was beginning to get on her nerves. "Greg, are the Basses pretentious snobs?"

"No. William wouldn't be friends with them if they were."

"That's what we needed to know." Jane grinned, satisfied with his answer. "Thank you, honey."

"I'm being dismissed." Winking at his sister-in-law, this good-natured man forced himself to appear dejected for her benefit. Greg could sense by the questions Mara asked that they were having a woman's discussion, and he was thankful for the chance to escape before they started asking him about jewelry, or some other feminine subject he had no desire getting caught up in.

"Thank you, Greg. Don't worry. I promise to come hound you later."

"See, problem solved."

"It's not that simple, Jane," Mara said letting out an exasperated breath. Mara looked into the full-length mirror that stood in the corner of Jane's bedroom, feeling as if her sister wasn't taking her anxiety seriously, but Jane had been able to get Mara the facts she needed, and the rest she would have to figure out on her own.

The reflection in the mirror suddenly became two, as Jane stood beside her. It was true that Jane wasn't a woman led through life by her emotions, but she wasn't cold-hearted, either. Jane could see that Mara still needed reassurance, and though she wasn't sure how to give that to her, she wanted to try.

"You like William, don't you?"

Nodding, Mara allowed her eyes to lock with her sister's. "Very much."

"I do, too. So *you* need a dress."

Leaving her side, Jane opened the door to her walk-in closet, and motioned her sister to join her. Inside the room, beautiful clothes hung neatly from a rod, separated from the scrubs Jane wore to work and class. Many of them still had price tags attached, waiting in reserve for when Jane would have leisure time to wear them.

Gently picking through her collection of dresses, she brought out a red sleeveless dress with a plunging neckline and held it up against

Mara. Her sister's frame could pull it off, but she wasn't sure how the color would work on her. Placing it to the side as a possibility, Jane continued her search until a little black slip dress caught her attention.

"This is perfect." Jane had been saving it for when she and Greg went out on the town, but frankly, she doubted that would be anytime soon, or at least not until after she graduated. Looking at the dress with the sentimentality she had attached to it, Jane realized that as much as she loved it, Mara would be stunning if she wore it. The dress was seductive without being vulgar, and the cut would certainly flatter her curves.

In an instant, her decision was made, and Jane handed her sister the hanger. "We're about the same size. Try this one on."

Mara complied with her request while Jane waited outside the closet, and when Mara emerged, Jane saw that she had made the right selection for her.

"Take it. That dress was made for you. "

"I can't," Mara replied as she stared at herself in the mirror. How one dress could transform a person, Mara didn't know, but the effect it had on her was incredible. "I appreciate the offer, but you haven't even worn it yet, and if something should happen to it—.

"No, I mean it. Take it as a gift."

Gazing down at the price tag, Mara shook her head. "Jane, it's too expensive."

"Let me have some fun!" Jane ripped off the tag and put it in her pocket, experiencing how good it felt to do this for Mara. Taking her sister by the shoulders Jane spun Mara around so she was facing the mirror again. "Think about it. With a dress like this, it's goodbye schoolteacher, and hello goddess. How could you not want to wear this out with William? It's perfect. He'll love you in it."

Rolling her eyes at Jane's statement, Mara peered again at her reflection. She wanted the dress, and was leaning toward allowing her sister to give it to her when Jane came up with the perfect excuse that Mara couldn't refuse.

"Mara, it's a present. Happy early birthday!" Jane laughed. "Now, you need shoes, and I have a lot of those."

"Are you sure, Jane?"

"Positive."

Greg had been right to flee the scene while he had the chance, because the Bartlett sisters fell into makeover mode once Mara agreed to accept the present. Designer high-heeled shoes were scattered all over the room, handbags were thrown on the bed, and the merits of the waterbra over the demi push-up were discussed at length with a degree of seriousness most men would have difficulty justifying.

"What do I do with my hair?" Mara asked as she pulled it away from her face while Jane experimented on her with dark eye shadow.

"When in doubt, go with a loose bun at the nape of your neck." Her decided tone was enough for Mara to take her suggestion as gospel.

An hour later, Mara was set to leave for home with her head full of the tips her sister had given her and her hands full with her dress and accessories. Jane had been a godsend and given her an additional gift—confidence.

"I'm finally beginning to think I'm not in over my head." Mara told Jane at the door.

"You'll be beautiful."

The taxi had pulled away and Mara stood on the sidewalk with her suitcase in hand. She had the long train ride to think, and Mara fell into the trap of allowing herself to dwell on the doubts she thought she had banished from her mind. Peering up at the façade of William's brownstone, she immediately realized she was out of her element. One didn't require first hand knowledge of the Manhattan real estate market to recognize the property was worth more than she would earn in a lifetime.

The building was not ostentatious on the outside, only intimidating. The architecture, with its orderly yet impressive lines, was ageless. She imagined it appeared exactly as it was now one hundred years ago, when people drove up to it in their carriages.

Turning around, Mara faced the park across the street. It had obviously always been there, as the trees amongst the groomed landscape showed their age. A couple was jogging on the sidewalk in their perfectly coordinated warm up suits, and every sight she observed brought Mara closer to the conclusion that she did not belong there.

"Are you going to come in?" William asked, startling Mara. She hadn't noticed that he had opened the door and was standing in the doorway waiting for her. His smile was welcoming, and Mara forced herself to push aside her self-doubt. It threatened to overshadow her joy at being with William again.

Crossing into the foyer, Mara could feel his excitement by the way William's hand rubbed her back as she walked beside him. He tenderly kissed her as soon as the door was closed, and yet she felt herself pulling away from him as soon as it was over.

"Did you have any difficulty with the trip?" His eyes searched her face as he waited for Mara's reply.

"No, the directions you gave were great. There were no problems."

William took the suitcase handle she was clutching. Her attempt at casual discourse was not convincing, and Mara wasn't aware that she was speaking at a higher pitch than she usually did.

"Is something wrong?"

Shaking her head, she smiled. "I'm fine."

If you'll hand me your coat, I'll hang it up. Then I'll take you upstairs so you can unpack."

William spoke at length about the weekend he had planned for them as he removed a hanger out of the closet in the foyer. He had high hopes that he would be able to make it memorable for her, knowing that Mara's birthday was a week away, and he wouldn't be with her to celebrate it.

But the longer William talked, the more he became aware he was having a one-sided conversation. Mara answered his questions and made comments, but they rarely were more than monosyllabic replies. Realizing she might be nervous about her first visit to see him, especially after enduring a train, subway, and a taxi cab, William decided to postpone taking her up to unpack until she had a chance to relax.

"I'm glad you're here." Brushing her hair behind her ears, William duplicated the welcoming smile he had given her when he first saw her. "Do you want a tour of the downstairs, first?"

"That's up to you."

"Would you like a drink?"

"No. I mean yes." Her reply was tempered with a shyness Mara generally did not possess. "What ever you want will be good."

Once William got to the counter in the kitchen, he became aware that Mara hadn't followed him. That was when he started to question if there wasn't more to her standoffishness than he had originally thought.

William was last in Vermont only two weeks before for Valentine's Day, and if something had occurred between then and now to make Mara question this visit, she hadn't hinted at it during their many phone conversations.

After reminding himself that Mara had been uncharacteristically quiet the night before when he was giving her last minute directions about the train schedule, William wondered if he hadn't ignored warning signs that she was losing interest in him. How else could he explain her sudden change in disposition?

William had told her some things he hadn't shared with any other woman, secrets that even Greg didn't know, and when he was making love to her, William expressed himself completely and without inhibition. Mara brought out that part of him, by making him feel safe to be himself.

Mara wasn't the only one in their relationship with insecurities. William was wearing his heart on his sleeve when it came to her. Although they had not spent as much time together as he would have wanted, he was already finding that he needed contact with her daily. Mara was becoming that vital to him.

If she was changing her mind about being with him, or if the relationship was deteriorating, he would rather be told so now. He was not a man that liked guessing, nor was he one who put stock in the adage that everything will work itself out. William did better dealing in certainty.

When William returned with a wineglass in hand, Mara was standing exactly where he had left her, and he took that as a sign that she held no great curiosity in getting acquainted with his home.

"This is a big…" Mara raised her hands up to indicate she was making reference to the brownstone. "What do you call it?"

"Home." William replied flatly as he handed her a glass of wine.

Mara knew she was behaving strangely and that if she wasn't careful, William might misconstrue her actions, but she couldn't figure out how to seem self confident, when every time she looked around, she felt like she was intruding.

Logic couldn't calm her fears, and neither could reminding herself that William wouldn't have invited her to New York had he not wanted her to come. The little farmgirl that still lived inside of Mara, who never thought she was clever or pretty enough to compete with the girls from town, haunted her from time to time.

"Mara, do you want to leave?" she heard William say, and recognizing he felt as though he needed to ask the question made Mara's stomach turn.

"No."

"If you don't want to be here—."

"I don't want to leave."

Gaining the courage to raise her eyes to him, Mara wished that William could just read her mind and understand that *he* was not the problem, but that facing the reality of his life was. Mara was well aware that he was wealthy, and she had accepted that, but now that it was shown to her in material form, her reaction was not what she had expected.

"Then please explain to me what's wrong and don't hold back."

"I didn't realize that you lived like this. I've been taking you to diners in town, and to my parents' farm…God, I took you to the vet's office with me one morning."

"So?"

"Look at this place, William. This is intimidating."

"What is?"

"All of this."

"Would it have made a difference had you known before? Would it have stopped you from getting involved with me? "

"I don't think so."

William had never imagined that this would be an issue for them. He had been straightforward with Mara about who he was, or at least William thought he had. He had gone to her parents' house for lunch and—.

Then in a moment of clear thought, William understood what she was really telling him. He, too, had felt out of place, even intimidated, when he had been at her parents' home by the way the family interacted with each other. It had been foreign to him and more uncomfortable than he had anticipated.

"Let me show you something. Come with me." Taking the wineglass from Mara's hand and placing it on a table, William laced his fingers with hers and walked her over to a lighted display case. "Your mother has your grandmother's china displayed in her dining room, right?"

"Yes."

"Well, this was my grandmother's vase collection."

Pointing up to the wall, William continued. "Over here is a portrait of my parents, painted from their wedding picture."

Mara stared at the painting for some time, fascinated by the resemblance William held to his father. She caught herself glancing between William and the portrait, comparing similarities and differences. With her hand still in his, the tour continued.

"The table under the portrait is one my grandfather bought when he was England during the war. He had it shipped here as a gift to his mother."

Stepping closer, Mara noticed that the only piece displayed on the table was a small metal trophy. It seemed out of place against the splendor of the marble top of the table.

"That was an award my father earned for his fundraising efforts for The New York Institution for the Blind. He received it the year after we were diagnosed. He worked hard for it."

Mara knew that the Institute was one of William's most treasured clients, simply by the respectful manner in which he spoke about the work he did for them, but until now, she hadn't known that he was the second generation of his family to take up their cause.

Grasping his hand tighter, Mara turned away from the simple trophy and really looked at William as he was in his own home. Dressed in jeans, a white button down shirt with the sleeves rolled up, and a navy blue sweater vest, he didn't seem out of place amongst the possessions that surrounded him. And yet, he didn't appear any different than when he was in Vermont.

Mara was starting to acknowledge that she had allowed herself to get worked up over imaginary obstacles, giving them permission to fester in her mind until they had actually become real obstacles for her to contend with.

William and Mara made a complete round of the living room. Not every item was an antique or highly prized. It was much like her own home, where some of her most prized pieces were the least valuable.

"Does it make a difference to who I am that I have all of this, Mara?" William asked, with a look that showed he adored her. If his explanations took away some of the intimidation Mara had confessed, then he would spend the rest of the night showing her around so that she could be herself again. He didn't want to lose her over this.

"No. It doesn't matter." Finally, Mara was beginning to become comfortable in William's home. What the brownstone held inside its walls was his history, and that was something she wanted to know all about.

"I've missed you." William was serious, despite the happiness reflected in his eyes.

He lowered his head and kissed her. It was William's intention for it to be a brief expression of how glad he was that she had come to Manhattan, but best intentions can sometimes go astray when a woman enchants a man.

William began kissing her as he preferred when they were alone and without the constraints of time—slow and passionate with deliberate movements and tender pressure. All of the restrained longing came out as his lips glided their way over Mara's, and the sensations created were electric.

Her mouth was as soft and warm as he had remembered, as he tried to replace the two-week-old memory from the last time they kissed, with a new one. A throaty gasp from her urged him on. It was incredible the way Mara made him feel alive. And yes, it was possible to make love to someone with only a kiss, because William was proving it.

The next evening in New York, Mara Bartlett danced for the first time with William Grant under the sultry influence of the blues. She had the time of her life with him, swaying to the music with their lips rarely straying from each other. Envious eyes fell on the couple who didn't disguise their desire for each other, strangers wondering what their secret was to happiness.

Neither were exhibitionists and William was keenly aware of where his hands were while they were in the club, but his mind was not so courteous. Since the moment Mara had come out of his room dressed for the evening in her little black dress, William couldn't wait to take her out of it. He had always thought Mara was beautiful, but this night she was absolutely sexy.

Despite his urgency to have Mara all to himself, they met his friends at the club. The Basses were exactly as Greg had described them to Mara—nice people. They all enjoyed their time together, and when William and Mara headed back to his home around one in the morning, they were tired but sharing the same thoughts about the rest of the night.

After William hung up their coats in the foyer, life reentered his weary limbs while Mara's lips played against his as he leaned against the closet door, and the fine line between love and lust began to fade into a despondency that could only find solace in body.

His hands moved deliberately down her body to rest on her hips, a place they had longed to touch all evening, as her warmth radiated through the thin material stretched across her. Then basic sensual need commanded William as it had never done before.

William met the challenge by lifting her from the floor and into his arms so they were facing each other, her body weight pressing against the rapidly growing erection he knew she could feel against her abdomen.

"I need you." He whispered hoarsely. Mara responded by wrapping her legs tightly around him, her eyes intense with equal want. Lust would reign the victor this night as the zipper on the back of her dress was lowered so that the straps fell from her shoulders.

"Perfect, Mara." William breathed, his body on fire. His mouth came down hard on hers. His fingers worked their way under the material that separated Mara's skin from his touch, until his palms tingled from the friction as they ran the length of her back.

"Right here," Mara slid from his embrace causing the dress to pool around her high heels, then she began undressing him—only what was needed for their immediate satisfaction. From William's wallet she took a condom, a necessity he had begun carrying since they began dating.

Once again William raised Mara up, and she reached down and took hold of him in preparation for him to enter her very willing flesh. As he lowered her onto himself, William lost his breath for several seconds; his mouth parted as the sensation of her tightly enveloping him took away the primal need for oxygen.

When air again entered his lungs, it was labored and a secondary instinct to the necessity for release. Without needing instruction, Mara began a rocking motion with her hips, her hands linked behind his neck.

She knew exactly what she was doing—she was driving William over the edge and the power of the act itself heightened her gratification. Mara rested her open mouth on the place behind his ear where she could feel his pulse beat against her moistened lips. He made the mistake of telling her how sensitive that area was to her touch and she took advantage of the knowledge.

William responded as she expected, with an urgency to bring her body down harder on his for several strokes until he told her to stop. 'No' was her answer, and his end was near.

"I'm close—" William moaned, balancing on that edge where sexual pleasure was most intense. His forewarning did nothing but encourage her. He shuddered and held Mara close to him as his body emptied all of its reserves into her; the force of his release was so powerful that it was painful for them both.

William's head arched back to rest against the door with his neck extended and eyes closed. It was the single most profound orgasm he had ever experienced. Made up of his craving for her in every way. Time stood still until his senses returned, and once fully realized, William had but one design in mind. That was to return the favor.

A week later the phone began to ring in her house. Mara looked down at her watch and smiled to herself.

"Hello," she assumed it could be no one else but William on the other end of the line. Six weekends had been spent together since that first one of being snowed in at Greg's, and certain rituals had already developed.

"Hello, yourself. I've been thinking about you all day. What are you doing?" Settling into his desk chair, William smiled, grateful for the invention of the telephone. The distance between where they lived proved to be more of an inconvenience than a hindrance, eased by their nightly conversations.

Although it was never discussed, it was taken for granted that they were seeing each other exclusively. Mara had found her way into his heart without trying, and she was now very much a part of him. William never thought his life was empty before she entered it—quiet, but not empty.

Then he met Mara, and the contentment she brought to him was a gift he wanted to give back to her. It was the aspect of being a couple that encouraged him to reevaluate what he held private, and over time William's sharing parts of himself was becoming habit and natural, never forced.

"I just finished grading tests," she answered him. "And you?"

"I was thinking about coming to Vermont this weekend. Are you free?"

"Yes! Remember, I have a long weekend." William had remembered and purposely cleared his schedule to extend his trip. "Would you take the Friday night train?"

"What if I took the Friday morning?" he countered.

"Even better! I'll pick you up at the station. Will you stay with me this time? Say yes, William. We're not fooling anybody. You always end up here, no matter how sly we try to be."

"I'll have to think on your offer and get back to you. I'm in very high demand in Vermont."

William was becoming quite accomplished at teasing her, which she encouraged at every opportunity. Few people who claimed familiarity with William would say that he was a humorous man, but then again, few people really knew him as Mara did.

"I don't think you'll have to consider your options for long." Mara laughed before her tone decidedly changed. "I guess I should warn you now that I'll be having my period this weekend."

"I don't care." William was telling the truth. "What would you like to do?"

They talked it over and decided to take Greg and Jane out to dinner on Saturday night, and when Mara had to go back to teach school, William would spend time the day with his friend before returning home.

"When I get there Friday, I want to go somewhere we haven't been before. What about the farmer's market you told me about?"

"I really think you'd like it. Oh, before I forget, they've asked me to do summer school this year. It's only for a month.

"When would it be?" William had more than one reason for his question.

"Some of June into July. But I'd be off from then until the very end of August."

"Perfect. Would you let me take you somewhere this summer?"

"Do you have a particular place in mind?"

"What about Hilton Head Island?"

"Really?"

"My family owns a house on the beach, and I have it for the last two weeks in July." The idea of the two of them spending time in South Carolina without any responsibilities or distractions had been on William's mind for a while.

"William, is this a country club setting you're talking about?"

"No. Just a house on the beach." William went on to explain that when he had been there in the past, he preferred to stay on the water. It was very secluded—it would be a perfect get-away for the two of them.

His descriptions must have been alluring because Mara agreed to go with him to South Carolina in July. Her thoughts ran very much like his, and the temptation of two weeks alone was too great to pass up.

After they said their goodbyes, William turned off his phone, feeling as if the best part of the day had just passed. He and Mara had slowly increased their phone conversations until they became a ritual of every evening at seven and occasionally throughout the day, if they had something of interest to share.

William would always call, and at first, Mara had resisted, but he made up a pathetic excuse about working odd hours and told her it was easier for him. In truth, William didn't want her to run up a phone bill, and although Mara could be as stubborn as he was, she did relent this once.

He was proud of the way she earned her own way in life. Occasionally, it did get in their way during those times when he wanted to provide for her. There was the time William had taken her to a benefit he had to attend, and Mara wouldn't let him buy her an outfit, but he respected her integrity, even when he didn't get his way.

William never imagined himself falling in love with a woman as absolutely as he had Mara, and although he tried to live in the moment, there were indicators that the future was gaining on him with a certainty he dreaded.

Placing the phone on his desk, William turned on the large flatscreen computer monitor, pulling up the word processing program he used. The screen went black with white lettering in a large font, the size of which had been increased for the second time in a month. Despite this change, William continued to strain his eyes to make out what was before him.

The change in his sight was a subject William tended to avoid. He didn't talk about his doctor appointments or the subtle variations in his vision that he had been noticing lately. It was selfish on his part, and he did recognize that, but the underlying fear William associated with his situation was more pronounced than the still, small voice inside of him that told him he needed to talk to her about it.

He would be seeing Mara—figuratively and literally—in three days, and at that moment, it was all that mattered to him. He would tell her about the changes soon.

After the train stopped at Mara's station, William waited for the others to depart before rising from his seat. Folded in his coat pocket was the cane he brought with him. Twice he had to use it on the trip from Manhattan because the bright sunlight was wreaking havoc with his ability to see, but he was confident he could complete this last leg of the journey without it. Walking down the isle, William heard her say his name from the opposite direction he was headed.

They rode to Mara's house in the new car he had helped her pick out on his last visit. William had never driven in his life, but when the time came for negotiating the price, he was extremely useful as the salesman tried to take advantage of her by selling multiple warranties that essentially covered the same thing.

Their relationship was one of give and take, of opposites that complimented each other. Mara drove, and William cooked. She educated children, and he influenced adults. She worked for her money, and he had inherited his. Where one might have a weakness, the other often compensated with their strength, and this was what made them a strong couple. They had learned to respect each other's differences.

Once they were inside, Mara told William she had rearranged some of her furniture so that it was more intuitively placed. William's first comment was that she didn't have to accommodate him, but Mara reminded William that he had gone out of his way to make her feel at home when she was in New York.

"Moving the kitchen table and a few footstools isn't disruptive. It's common courtesy—like when you get me whole milk when I stay at your place." Mara took hold of his hand. "The idea is the same."

"You're right." Her argument was sound, and William conceded without any more discussion.

"And I have good news for you."

"What's that?"

"Mother Nature is being kind by holding off on *the curse*. If you come with me now, we can take advantage of her generosity."

She stood in front of him unbuttoning his shirt while he sat on the couch, but the enthusiasm William usually displayed wasn't there.

"All right, William. What's on your mind?" Mara asked quietly as she rested her forehead against his.

Mara's statement about her period being late left William numb and terrified, and it was not a discussion that he could put off until later. What he needed her to understand would be difficult for him to say because of his deep conviction on the subject. William wouldn't only be addressing this month, but on an unconditional level, every month thereafter.

"Mara, we need better protection than the condoms we're using. It needs to be thoroughly foolproof."

"Why?"

"Do you understand what autosomal dominant means?" William was referring to a term in genetics.

"Yes. Is that the classification of retinitis pigmentosa you have?"

"It is."

"Have you done genetic counseling?"

"Yes," he admitted nervously. What William had was an inherited trait, and if he ever fathered a child, it would be passed on to the baby, giving it a one in two chance of having his disorder.

"And you want to take every precaution?" Mara was too intelligent not to grasp what he was talking about and the long-term implications involved, if she was to stay with him. William was essentially letting her know that he would never willingly father children.

"I do."

"Next week I'll have Jane start me on a more reliable form of birth control."

"No, I'll take care of it myself. It needs to be done."

"Whether you do that or not doesn't matter. I'm still going to see Jane next week." Mara moved to sit on his lap. "Now, I have something to tell you."

"What is it?"

"Last night I took a pregnancy test because I was worried about being late. It was negative. We really are just getting a lucky break."

If there was ever an opening for William to speak freely about his expectations for the future, it was at this moment, but he didn't know where to start.

"You're making all the sacrifices, Mara."

"No, I'm not. I looked up what you have long before I kissed you for the first time, and I knew what I was getting into."

Mara was more at peace in the three months she had been with William than she had been in years. He was a remarkable lover and an excellent friend, and through his eyes, she was beginning to see the good in herself that had been hidden from her for a long time.

With the love she had never spoken aloud, Mara reassured him. "I'd walk across fire just to pick up the phone to hear you ask me how my day was going. You give me so much more than I could—."

William covered Mara's mouth with his own as her words sank in. They didn't change William's conviction that she had to conform to be with him, but it did soothe his mind that Mara was aware when she entered into their relationship.

The next words to come from William expressed what he honestly felt for her. "I love you."

Smiling against his cheek, Mara returned the sentiment. "I love you, too, Will."

His smile soon matched hers, and these two people who had been thrown together by luck admired the other who had won their heart. Mara could see that William loved her, and recognized it when he touched her face, but when they melted together on the couch with his lips touching hers, Mara was convinced of it.

Stretched out with arms and legs entwined, William broke away from her mouth. With the weight of his body pressing against hers, he asked in a hoarse voice, "I guess that means we can blow off the trip to the farmer's market?"

"Oh yeah."

Hand in hand they went up the staircase to her bedroom, the brightness from outside kept at bay by the curtains covering the windows, yet there was sufficient light to make out the forms and outlines of the bodies that would soon be united together. William touched her softly on the small of her back, and the slow undressing of each other commenced.

With her fingertips skimming his bare chest, any modesty exhibited when they entered the room dissolved as William pulled the cover from the bed. Trust united them now, and the newly expressed love made Mara feel like it was their first time together.

Skin against skin, he covered her with the heat radiating from his body. The day was indeed young and neither displayed an urgency to surrender to the passion building within them. It *was* different this time, and both felt it.

"Tell me you're mine," he murmured as a hand cupped a breast and his eyes met hers.

"You know I am." Mara was not a woman to do anything by halves. Either she gave her all or none. When she realized she was in love with William, it was completely and without hesitation. She was his equal in devotion. "I love you so much."

Looking down at the woman who held him spellbound, William moved alongside her on the bed so he could indulge in the touch of her body. The silkiness of Mara's skin skimmed under his fingertips, and every caress marked the trail William effortlessly created followed down her hip.

With the provocative parting of her legs, an invitation was issued. William watched as her eyelids fell shut before she tensed up, the faint essence of her sex perfuming the air, invoking an ancient response in him.

William's breaths turned ragged in time with hers, and he felt the heat between her legs increase as he concentrated on the spot that provoked her moans and caused his erection to swell. Words were said that only lovers exchange as Mara neared her peak, and when her hand reached out to grip his head, William knew she was about to climax.

The depth of the contractions that rocked her body astonished him, and before they ended, William positioned himself over her. Mara wrapped her legs around his waist and guided him in, and he experienced the remaining remnants of her orgasm tighten around him and instinct overrode reason.

Feeling utterly complete, senses awoke in William on every level. He caught himself holding his breath as he entered her as far as her body would allow, the nails digging into his back going unnoticed as he withdrew and entered her again. It was a sensation that could never be repeated enough.

Sweat glistened on his back as blood coursed through his veins. The need was unyielding in its demand to be satisfied, a burning unrelenting to feel the cradle of Mara's body. A part of his mind told him to slow down and make it last, but when Mara cried out his name as she came close again to her own fulfillment, William lost that control as his own descent was initiated with a decisive rush of blood to his sex.

"I love you," he admitted seconds before the first spasm ripped through him, all movement ceasing as an overpowering sensitivity to touch temporarily immobilized him. Then another wave hit, and continued until William's body was completely spent.

Afterwards, Mara rested with her head on his chest listening to his heartbeat while his hand stroked her thigh. As they fell asleep, the afternoon sun began to set.

That night Mother Nature paid a call on Mara, but not until they had finished celebrating once again saying those three precious words to each other.

Spring
~~..~~

Chapter Four

~~..~~

Weeks turned into months, and before they knew it, the slumber of winter had passed and May had arrived.

The alarm woke William out of his deep sleep, and as he reached over to nudge Mara so she could turn it off, the memory that she had gone back to Vermont the night before returned to him. Blindly reaching out for the snooze bar, William laid there with his eyes closed, as he drifted within the semiconscious state of wakefulness.

He could smell the traces of her perfume that still lingered on his pillowcase, but when he touched the side of the bed Mara slept on with his palm, it was a cold reminder that she was gone. Another two weeks would have to pass until William would be able to see her again.

For the next few minutes, he allowed his mind to replay scenes from the weekend they had just spent together. She had arrived early on Friday and that night, William was able to take her to her first play in New York. She had chosen Shakespeare, which William would have never guessed, but that was what she asked for, and he had been able to get tickets.

Mara was a closet romantic. She kept ticket stubs and napkins and little mementos of where they had been together in a box at home. She told William about it, but had never shown it to him. On the weekends she was in New York, William spent contributing to her collection.

Since the day he told her that he loved her, William experienced a change come over him. He started thinking more about the future and what he had to offer a woman as rare as he found Mara to be. He had loved her months before he told her, the hesitation brought on by his concern that once she knew what sort of future he faced, including the absence of biological children if she stayed with him, she might consider the cost too great.

William had money, but it couldn't buy everything he wanted, as he had told her that first night at Greg's when they had talked. It couldn't buy him time. If he could have any wish, it would be for him to take Mara away and show her all he had seen in his lifetime—the cities, the places he had been as a child, the landmarks he had looked upon. But she would never agree. William would even send her back to college, if that was what she truly wanted. It didn't matter to William. He had come to realize that his own happiness was directly tied to hers, and that was a part of love.

Love was also frightening, because it placed them in a position of dependence, and although he could live with the idea, it was the vulnerability for both of them that worried him. William trusted Mara, but how much was he willing to ask her to sacrifice to be with him? That was the question that William always came back to. Mara's vitality fed him, and yet, was that in her best interest? Would she get to a point where she began to think of him as a burden?

William had seen that happen before.

These were the heavy questions that clouded his mind as the alarm went off a second time. Melancholy didn't suit him, and it wasn't a state in which he often found himself. Just occasionally William would venture to the dark corners of his mind, before he would remind himself that Mara loved him as he was. It was an injustice for him to group her with the others, whose fidelity was bound with conditions based on factors over which he had no control.

Turning the alarm off, William rubbed his face before opening his eyes. The room was dark, and it took him a moment before he became orientated. Believing that Mara must have reset the clock incorrectly, he brought it next to him to press the button that spoke the time aloud. It said seven twelve in the morning.

Knowing that was wrong, William turned on the light on his nightstand, but it wasn't working. Wondering if a power surge had occurred after he went to bed, he rose and walked to the hallway. This problem had happened before, as the wiring in the home was older than he was, and William knew he needed to stop putting off fixing it and call the electricians.

Feeling his way down the wall, he found the switchplate for the hallway. He couldn't remember if it was on the same circuit as his bedroom or not. Again, William concluded that a fuse must have blown because after he flipped the switch, the light did not turn on.

Hearing the soft hum of his computer in the spare bedroom he used as an office, William went into the pitch darkness of the room and sat down in his chair. *Something* wasn't right, but he couldn't put his finger on it. The nightlights he had to illuminate the room weren't on, and he could not attribute this to Mara having made a mistake. She never turned them off because she knew he couldn't see at night without them.

On his desk there was another talking clock, and after a moment's indecision, he touched it. It said fourteen minutes past seven in the morning.

William's denial was strong as he turned on the radio to a morning program he listened to during the week. The program was in progress, but he didn't know if they ran reruns at night or not, so he waited. It was some time before one of the men mentioned the New York sun coming through the window of their studio on this Monday morning, and with that statement came hope that if William parted his own curtains, he too would see it.

When he did, there was no light.

Coherent thought aside, William made his way downstairs and opened his front door. He could hear the cars going down the avenue and bits of conversation from people from the park across the street, and still William could see nothing. This had never happened to him before—the complete absence of sight. Even on his worst days, there were always shadows and bright spots in which shapes could be made out.

In that moment he felt utterly alone, even though he was surrounded by the sounds of life coming from outside. Unable to move, he stood there with his hand gripping the doorknob, knowing that nothing would ever be the same again. William had felt this way before, when he had received the news that both of his parents had been killed. There were no second chances then, and in his gut he realized that there wouldn't be this time, either.

With his worst nightmare playing out while he was wide awake, William closed the door and took a step back. His denial was dissipating faster than his mind could keep up. Turning around, he walked into the livingroom, forgetting to count his steps and slamming his knee against the edge of the couch. Using his hands, he followed it down to where a table with a lamp was. As a final act, William turned on the lamp, picking it up at an angle where the light would surely be caught by his eyes.

There was no light.

Hours later, William stood in his ophthalmologist's office facing the wall with his arms crossed and his body gently rocking back and forth. His doctor had called in his colleague to confirm what he already had diagnosed. Neither man talked as they examined William's eyes, using every test at their disposal, although one look inside told them that it was hopeless.

"William," he doctor said. "It's too late. Surgery isn't an option. I can see evidence of minute blood clots that may have…"

"Call me a taxi." The details were no longer important to him.

"Do you have someone to stay with you?"

"Yes," William lied.

A woman from the office walked him outside and hailed a taxi. Once he was home, William went throughout the house unplugging every telephone he owned before locking himself in his bedroom. Only then did he mourn the loss of his eyesight.

The last week of school was going to prove particularly trying for Mara if she judged by how her Monday went. The teachers didn't want to be there anymore than the students, and trying to keep everyone occupied while they let time run out was more difficult than it should have been. Mara waited that night for William's call, but it never came. They rarely missed a day talking on the phone, even after spending the weekend together.

Assuming William must have had something important to do that he had forgotten to mention to her, she went to bed that night believing that he would call in the morning. Tuesday passed, and at eight in the evening, she dialed William's phone number, but no one answered. After fruitless attempts every half-hour, the last being near midnight, she called Greg.

With a sick feeling inside of her, Mara told her brother-in-law all she knew, drawing out of him a confession that he had also been trying to reach William.

"Call the police and have them go to his house," Mara demanded. "Greg, something's wrong."

"I can't. He's not a missing person. They won't do it."

"What if he's fallen or is sick?"

"William's housekeeper comes on Tuesdays. She would have found him. We already have this all worked out. If anything ever happens to William, Gladys is to call me first. I've been home all day, and the phone hasn't rung once."

"Then you call her, Greg!"

"I would, but I don't know her last name."

If Mara believed that Greg was unconcerned, she was dead wrong. Greg had left messages twice on William's answering machine that day, and it was uncharacteristic of his friend not to return them. Now that Greg had additional information from Mara that he had not been in contact with her for two days, his mind went into overdrive devising a plan about how he could get answers, so if Greg sounded unfazed by Mara's news, it was for her benefit only.

"Send someone over there! Or else I'm going myself."

"Calm down, Mara. It's not helping."

"If it were Jane, would you be calm?"

"Okay, let me get off the phone and check around. If you don't hear back from me in the morning, I'll leave you a message at the school."

"You'll let me know as soon as you hear anything?"

"Yes. But don't panic. William might have caught the virus that's been going around, or something like that."

"The second you know…"

"I will."

Mara didn't sleep at all that night. She tried to call Greg before she had to leave to teach, but he didn't answer, and Jane wasn't at the doctor's office. In between first and second period at school, Mara checked her voice mail. Finally her sister had left a message. Greg was in New York, he had spoken to William at his home, and she was told not to worry because he would contact her later in the day.

Knowing William was safe, Mara felt a weight had been lifted from her and she made it through the rest of her school day, falling asleep on her couch in the living room as soon as she made it home. She had questions, a lot of them, that she pushed aside in her mind until she had a chance to talk to William, but Jane had told her not to worry, and that was advice she would follow.

It was nine in the evening when Mara's phone finally rang, waking her up. The caller ID told her it was coming from William's number. Instantly alert, she picked it up.

"Are you all right?" She answered, bypassing a greeting. Mara was caught between relief and frustration, which was apparent in her tone, but when there was no response, her emotions turned to dread.

"Will?" Mara asked softly, not certain if it was him or Greg on the line with her.

"Yes?"

"What's wrong?"

"I'm sorry, Mara."

"Yes, you should have called me. I was worried about you. Are you sick?"

"No."

William's voice was not right. There was an empty, emotionless quality to it that Mara had never heard before, not even when he would talk about his parents. It served as a warning to her, that she was about to be told something she wouldn't want to hear.

"William, what are you sorry about? You can tell me."

"I can't see you anymore. Mara, it's time now. I need to let you go, so you can date other men."

Many scenarios about what had kept William from contacting her had run through Mara's mind during the past three days, but there was one avenue of possibility she had never considered. That was that he wanted to end their relationship.

"For what reason?" Confused as to where this had all come from, and if it was maybe a misunderstanding, she waited for William's explanation before she would allow herself to believe she had heard him correctly.

"It's for the better."

"Wait...I don't understand what happened. Why?"

"Mara, it's nothing you did." His reply was barely audible. "It's my fault."

"Don't give me that excuse. William, are you ending it with me?"

"It's not your fault."

"That won't work." His words were turning an unthinkable possibility into reality, and Mara needed clarification before her conscious mind would accept it. "I want a yes or no answer."

There was a long period of silence when all Mara could hear was the sound of William breathing. It was surreal to her that they were even having this conversation, when not the weekend before they were planning out their summer together. How something so irreversible could have occurred between then and now to change how William felt about her, Mara couldn't fathom, but she needed to know.

"William, are you ending it with me?"

"Yes."

Their conversation did not last a full minute. In that short span of time, two hearts were broken as William set Mara free.

* * *

Life continued on. That Saturday, Thomas and Barbara Bartlett celebrated their thirtieth wedding anniversary at a pavilion in the park. It had been planned for months beforehand by Mara and two of her aunts. Regardless of how hard she was taking her ended relationship with William, Mara had to attend.

Parking her car on the side of the road, Mara picked up the present she had sitting on the passenger seat and walked toward the crowd of relatives and friends congregated at the picnic tables. No one in her family except Jane and Greg knew what had occurred in her private life.

The light sweater Mara wore over her sundress didn't keep the chill away from her, but she had also been unable to sleep much since Wednesday. This, as much as the cool temperature physically affected her. She was devastated.

Jane worked her way past some friends of the family, meeting her sister half way across the grassy hill. Under the guise of carrying the present for Mara, she took it from her and suggested they stand by themselves for a minute.

"Don't ask me anything," Mara pleaded, doubting Jane had any idea how she felt. Her self-control was hanging by a thread, and one wrong word from Jane threatened to break the composure she was trying so diligently to hold onto.

"I won't," her sister promised.

Mara had relationships in the past that had ended for one reason or another, but none of those partings compared to what she was going through now. Mara had loved William completely, she still did, and the finality of the breakup was not something she was dealing with well. Mara had thought he was the *one* for her, and now she questioned how her judgment could have been so wrong. Did she miss clues he was sending her?

After William called her for the last time, Mara began to question everything she thought they had together. She tried to convince herself that it was only about the sex for him, but that was not an excuse Mara could believe no matter how much she wanted to. Perhaps she was a bit naive, but she knew how to recognize love.

He still haunted her, and try as she might, Mara couldn't erase his image from her mind. Repeatedly she told herself it was done, that there was nothing left for her to cry over, but he still had her heart, and she didn't know how to get it back. She was tired of the drama of it all, and tired of finding reminders of him. Every time she picked up something William had left at her home, it only tore open the wound she just wanted to heal.

Feeling Jane's arm loop through hers, she cast her sister a sad smile. Today was not the day to think about William.

Laughter coming from the pavilion captured both of the sisters' attention as they turned in unison to watch their parents entertain their guests. As children, these young women were blessed to have been raised in a stable home, with two parents who cared about them. It wasn't always perfect in the Bartlett household, and like other families, they had their share of tough times, but the family stood together.

Their father, with his sensible ways and callused hands, was no romantic. Yet he always kissed his wife when he left the house, and she would sit with him when he came in from the barns to eat his lunch. There was nothing extraordinary about Thomas and Barbara Bartlett, but those small acts of expressed love left an impression on their daughters.

"Thirty years. How did they do it?" Mara asked, not expecting her sister to answer. Love was a mystery, and its longevity never certain.

Shaking her head, Jane answered honestly. "I don't know."

"I don't see Greg."

"He's at his parents'." Looking straight into the eyes of Mara, Jane didn't elaborate on her husband's whereabouts. "I want you to listen to me."

"Okay."

"I want you to fake it today. You need to walk over to Mom and Dad, and put a smile on your face like you mean it. You only have to do this for an hour, and then you can leave if you want. I'll cover for you."

Uncertain whether to thank Jane or tell her that her offer was unnecessary, Mara opened her mouth to respond, but was cut off as Jane had more to say.

"If you're asked where William is, and I know you will be, tell them that he couldn't make it. You don't owe anyone an explanation."

"I can do that."

"I know you can. You're stronger than you give yourself credit for."

Greg didn't return home for nine days. Once he unpacked and had a long discussion with Jane, he phoned Mara to ask her to come over the next morning. He needed a good night's rest to clear his head so he could better decide what he was going to do about what he already knew and what Jane had just told him about her sister.

Mara had resisted any attempts by Jane to talk about William, but that turned out for the best since Jane was asked not to disclose whatever information she gained from her husband. That was the condition William set before he would allow Greg to enter his home.

"When do you start teaching summer school?" Greg questioned the woman before him who stood rigid with an unreadable expression on her face. Jane had warned him that this was how he was going to find her sister. Over the course of time, Mara's hurt had turned into anger.

"We start in four days."

"Are you looking forward to it?

"No." Shaking her head, Mara sat down in a chair across from Greg. She didn't notice the thick stack of papers he was holding in his hands.

"William and I have been friends…"

"I don't want to talk about him. I don't even know why I came," Mara interrupted with a coldness that left no room for misinterpretation.

"Will you let me say what I need to?"

"Not if it is about him." Mara turned away. "He wouldn't even tell me why he was done with me, and I just don't care anymore."

"It's not your fault." Greg had spoken those words with compassion, but it was wasted, since he had unknowingly quoted what William said before Mara had hung up on him.

"Please, Greg."

"No more, then." Seeing the definite end to that part of the conversation, Greg tried another approach. "I asked you over here for a selfish reason."

"What's that?"

"I need someone who knows my books to help me out. Christian Moore is going in a different direction. I was hoping you might read it, and let me know what you think. I made you a printed copy last night."

This was the first time he had ever offered to let Mara see his work in progress. She wanted to ask Greg why he was doing this— expecting her to be able to concentrate on anything other than her own unhappiness. Then she realized that she had to do it. She had devoted the lion's share of two weeks grieving over William leaving her, and with each day that passed, it wasn't getting any easier.

Mara knew she couldn't continue this way, absorbed in her own pity and pushing away others who were trying to help. Reading for Greg could be a step in the right direction, although her heart wasn't in it. Reminding herself for the umpteenth time that she needed to move on with her life, Mara squelched the refusal that lay on the tip of her tongue. If nothing else, reading might be a welcome distraction.

"I'm not your best choice for a critic right now."

"I'm fine with that."

"When do you want me to read it?"

"Today?" Greg smiled to cover his anxiousness. He felt like he was gambling at a high stakes craps table, and if he made a mistake, he could lose more than Mara. He could lose his friend, too.

"Will it take long? I really need to work on my lesson plans for class."

"Not too long."

"I'll do it."

The smile Greg still had on his face fell slightly as he handed the bundle of pages to Mara.

"I need to caution you that I'm not sure what I'm going to do with this text yet. I might work it into the next book, or it could be an idea that could be made into its own story. Also, it does deal with Simon."

"I don't know if I want to read about him." Mara had once told William that Simon reminded her of him, in that they shared some of the same characteristics. If what Greg handed her was about Simon, her feelings over William might taint her view.

"I'll wait outside." Not acknowledging Mara's hesitancy, Greg stood up to leave.

Staring down at the papers she had laid on her lap, Mara read the title. *For the love of Iliana.*

"Who's Iliana?" She called out before Greg was out of earshot.

"A new female character."

When she was finished, Mara went outside in search of her brother-in-law. He was in the backyard, sitting under an umbrella with a pen and pad of paper in his hand. The frost was gone from her demeanor, replaced with open admiration and contentment.

"It was impressive, Greg," she said as she handed him back the manuscript. "This is some of your best storytelling ever. I noticed variations from your typical writing, but it's obvious that you wrote it with a great deal of feeling. Simon could easily be a leading man, in my opinion, and you prove that with the richness of the descriptions you used."

"What did you think of Iliana?"

"She…she's interesting. I like her, and I'm not generally drawn to female characters. Her innocence disturbed me at first, because their world is so harsh and the weak don't survive long. But you gave her wisdom, and I could see how that balanced her inexperience. I hope you continue her character in the story. It was fascinating to watch how she interacted with Simon."

For the next fifteen minutes Mara gave a favorable review of what she had read, praising the beauty of the story itself. She talked until she was convinced Greg knew she was proud of him. He then made a special request.

"If I tell you a secret, will you swear that you'll never tell anyone else? Only five people know it, but it can't get out, Mara."

"Of course, I promise."

"As you know, I never do public appearances as Christian Moore. There are a couple of reasons for my choice, the most important being that I want to remain anonymous."

"I can understand that."

"Here's what you can't tell anyone. Christian Moore is actually two people. My partner wants absolutely no credit, and is even more adverse to the publicity than I am. How we split up our duties is that he creates the characters and their personalities, we both contribute to the development of the plot, and I do the writing to bring it together."

"I see," Mara replied cautiously, sensing that Greg's confession was not yet complete.

"But this," Greg held up the manuscript, "this he wrote entirely on his own. It was intended to be a gift…"

"Who's your partner?" Mara instinctively knew the answer before she asked, although until this time she had never suspected.

"William."

Mara was rendered speechless as she thought about the man she still loved, coupled with the revelation from Greg. She had no idea that he wrote, let alone worked side by side with Greg, creating stories she had fallen in love with long before she knew the author.

"Why didn't he ever say anything to me?"

"He wasn't finished yet." Greg picked up the manuscript and put it in front of her. "This was intended to be the way William told you about it. He's been working on it for months. It was going to be a gift."

"I didn't know him at all."

"That's not true."

"He kept his writing secret from me."

"No, you're looking at it all wrong. William was writing it for you."

The tears that fell against Mara's cheeks went unchecked as she was torn between wishing that Greg had never disclosed his secret and experiencing the emotion William had written through the characters in his text. It was a step backwards, as far as she was concerned, for her to feel anything but anger at the man who broke her heart.

She had tried to convince herself that she did not care about him, that she could stop loving William as he had done to her, but the emptiness he left her with reminded Mara that she was only lying to herself.

There was no closure, and it felt more like a death to her rather than dissolution of a relationship. No one, including William, had explained to Mara why he no longer wanted to be with her, and as her questions went unanswered, she had convinced herself it was something she had done.

Mara shared this with Greg, speaking honestly and without restricting herself, which in turn prompted her brother-in-law to take matters into his own hands.

"I promised him I would not *tell* you why William did what he did," Greg stood and motioned toward the house. "Come with me, and I'll show you."

"Show me what?"

"Come with me." They both went back into the house, and Greg led Mara to the kitchen pantry.

"This room will work." He said as he turned on the light and invited her in, before closing the door behind him. Then Greg turned the light off.

"What do you see?"

"Nothing." The room was dark. Mara held her hand up near her face, but she couldn't make out the shape.

"In the older stories, Simon has the ability to heal himself, as you know, but he maintains his loss of vision as a reminder of the damage he can do. In William's manuscript, the character continues to deny his sight, even though he feels his blindness is a burden for Illiana. There are twenty more pages I haven't shown you because I don't like the changes William made. You see, he has Simon breaking his ties with Iliana because he is certain he will hold her back from her potential, and she will in turn resent him. I believe William drew from his own past history to write those pages."

"Why am I standing in here?"

"I can't answer that due to the promise I made not to *tell* you. Mara, what do you see in here?"

Once again she replied, 'nothing.' This was obviously Greg's way of telling her that something serious had happened to William's sight.

"How much vision does William have left?"

"I can't say, Mara. Just look around this room, because there's your answer."

"When did it happen?"

"It had to have been during those days he didn't call you."

Under the protection of darkness, Mara's emotions once again changed. Gone were the hurt, anger and denial that she had allowed to take control of her, and in their place stood a woman filled with resolve. This was the most important lesson her parents passed on to her—that when you love someone, you don't give up on them.

Armed with the truth that Mara had been shielded from, she knew what needed to be done.

"How's William doing?"

"Not well. This has hit him hard, and he wasn't ready for it. William hasn't told his family yet."

"He doesn't have to go through this alone."

"I know." Greg turned back on the light. "William's been my friend since we were nine. I can't do much more for him because he won't let me."

"If William wanted to come here, would you help him?"

"Yes, Jane and I have already discussed that. He's not close to his family in New York. They're a different kind of people, and their priorities are deeply embedded in appearances. But Mara, I've already tried."

Mara exited the pantry and looked up at the clock on the wall. She didn't need Jane to borrow courage from, she had her own.

"There's a train to New York in two hours. Will you take me to the station?"

"I will. Why don't you go home and pack? I'll pick you up."

As Mara was about to leave, Greg gave her one more piece of information he thought she needed to know.

"William believed he was doing what was best for you. You have to remember that when you see him."

"He was wrong."

There were three houses on the country road Mara turned down as she went home to pack. Her family's farm, her uncle's farm, and the small two-story house she rented. The white metal fence that lined her father's property was a blur as she drove by it, but at the last minute, she slowed down and turned left on to the gravel drive that led to the house and barns.

She wanted to let her folks know at least where she was going, and stopping by wouldn't take much more time than calling. Bypassing the house, Mara pulled her car up to the barn where she thought she had her best chance of finding her father. The tanker truck that was usually parked beside it was gone, which meant that the morning milk collection was over, and the man they had working for them was on the road. If she was lucky, Mara would find her father alone.

Walking down the corridor between the pens where the cattle were milked everyday, she recalled how William once told her that it was more industrial than he had expected. But it had to be kept clean, for even though the guidelines for food sanitation were strict, her father was stricter. His reputation was on the line.

At the end of the walkway, she spied her father hunched over a piece of machinery with a wrench in his hand. Dressed in his jeans and a flannel shirt, Mara didn't think he looked like a man of fifty-seven, but then again, when it came to her daddy, she only saw the good.

"Hey, kiddo. Did you come to help your old man today?"

"Sorry, Dad, but no." Mara smiled, certain that he'd put her to work if she stayed too long. "I came to tell you I'm going to New York for a few days."

"Did you and William make up?"

"Not exactly."

Placing the wrench next to his project, Thomas stood up. He wasn't a man who dispensed his advice lightly, but he was protective of his girls. If the thought that one of them was about to make a mistake, other than the usual lessons people had to learn in life, Thomas would tell them.

"Why are you going?"

"William's in trouble."

Mara could not tell her father everything that she knew, in part because Greg asked her not to, but she could give her father enough information about William that the frown he was wearing was replaced by an expression of concern.

It was no secret that Thomas was fond of William, and that he treated him like he did Greg—as if he were already a part of the family. He had even taken him into his workshop, which was a sure sign that Thomas approved of someone.

He liked the young man because William had taken the time to get to know him and his wife. That said a lot to Thomas about his integrity. Boyfriends that hid from the girl's parents were never any good in Thomas' book, and though that might seem like simple logic, it generally was right on the money.

After Mara explained that William had lost all of his sight, and that Greg had told her that he wasn't doing well, the sense of urgency Mara had experienced upon hearing the news was shared by her father. He wanted her to go because he had faith she could do some good.

"You take care of yourself," Thomas nodded, damn proud of this eldest. "I'll keep an eye on your house while you're gone. Call me if you need anything."

"Thanks, Dad."

Kissing him on the cheek, Mara started to leave. Her explanation hadn't taken very long, leaving her plenty of time to pack and close up her house before Greg came to pick her up.

"Mara?" Feeling her dad grasp her arm, she turned around.

"Yes?"

"When I found out about my cancer, I didn't take it well. I was cross with your mother, and worried about you kids, the farm, and who was going to take it over if something happened to me."

Mara remembered that period in their lives very well. It had taken her father a while to adjust, and during that period, he didn't act like the man that had raised her.

"You might find that, when you're there with William. It sounds like he's going through a real bad time. Just don't forget that he's a good guy underneath it."

"I won't."

Reaching into his back pocket, Thomas pulled out his wallet and opened it, removing several bills. "Take this."

"Dad, I don't need money."

"Take it. It makes me feel like I'm doing something."

There was no use arguing with the man. Taking the money in her hand, Mara gave her father another kiss on the cheek and told him that she loved him. "Will you tell Mom that I'm gone? But don't tell her why. She'll just stew about it."

"I'll take care of it."

Summer

~~..~~

Chapter Five

~~..~~

Across the street from where William lived, Mara sat on a bench with a backpack slung over her shoulder and her cell phone in hand. She had just hung up with Greg, who after a series of calls, found out that William wasn't at home. According to William's housekeeper, Gladys, he was expected to return soon.

Gladys had agreed to allow Mara inside when she arrived, although she had reservations. She had been working for William's family since he was a young boy, and Gladys knew she was betraying her loyalty by taking part in the intervention Greg had proposed to her. But she was convinced that the despondency William exhibited was progressively becoming worse, and this concern prompted her to agree to Greg's request that should Mara need to be admitted into the home she would have Gladys' cooperation.

It really wasn't necessary, since Greg had slipped Mara his key to William's door before she left, but it was a comfort for the both of them to know Mara had an ally. She would need it.

Mara had absolutely no plan of what she was going to say or do when she saw William, and she wouldn't allow herself to think on that fact while she waited for him, instead opting to rely solely on instinct to lead her. For forty minutes, she sat outside until a taxi stopped in front of William's brownstone, and then the man she would know anywhere got out.

Two differences caught her attention right away. William was not wearing his sunglasses, which had been a mainstay before, and he opened up a cane once he stepped away from the cab. That was when reality hit her, and Mara began berating herself for her arrogance to think she had the qualifications to even reach out to him.

Faith in oneself is often a fragile belief, and Mara's was wavering. Her analytical mind overrode the messages coming from her heart, but there was one truth that she knew for certain—William did not want her there. He did not want her to know he was completely blind and had determined that Mara would now consider him a burden.

Mara was not one who took kindly to others making decisions for her, even when they thought that they were protecting her. Her innate independence rose to the challenge as her father's wisdom sang out like a siren's call. If William truly did not care for her anymore, Mara would accept that, but by God he was not going to go through this alone.

Mara would be the one to decide if she wanted to share this with him, and no one, including William, had the right to make that choice for her. Granted, her logic was as flawed as his, since Mara gave no consideration to William's desires, but it was what motivated her to cross the street. Strength, even when it was misguided, was still strength.

Once William was inside, Gladys came to look for Mara, and when she spotted her, waved for her to come over. There was not a lot to be said between them. Gladys wanted to remain as neutral as possible, and only the older woman's hand on her shoulder told Mara that she wished her the best. Once she crossed the threshold into William's home, Mara knew there was no turning back.

"He's in his bedroom," Gladys told her as she retrieved her purse from a table in the foyer, leaving Mara alone. After the front door was closed and locked, Mara's gaze went to the stairway leading to the second story. The last time she had been here, William had chased her up them, laughing as she had coaxed him with a reward if he could catch her.

Now Mara climbed the steps with a slow, fixed pace, holding tightly to the handrail and without any eagerness to reach his bedroom as quickly as possible. She knocked lightly before opening the door, looking toward the bed for him. William wasn't there, and the door had to be opened wider for Mara to see that he was sitting in a wing chair across the room.

His appearance did not give her the impression of good health. William had obviously lost weight, but perhaps more than that, it was the inexpressive cast to his face which made him look unwell.

"Gladys, why don't you go on home? I don't want dinner tonight and can take things from here," he offered gently.

The guilt associated with the fact that Mara was catching William unaware was strong. He had no means to prepare himself, and that made her realize she was taking advantage of his situation. There was no other recourse, Mara had to speak, but she already felt as if she had made her first mistake.

"Gladys has already left, Will. And yes, you do need some dinner. You're getting too thin."

William did not move except to close his eyes. Whatever his inner reaction was, outwardly he didn't move.

"Is Greg here?" was all William said to mark her presence. His shock at hearing the sound of Mara's voice left him confused, and after a brief moment, he wasn't certain it really was her. It could have been Jane, or his cousin, Anne.

"No," Mara's own voice cracked, "just me, William."

"Mara, please leave," he pleaded, as quietly as he had spoken when he thought Gladys had entered his room.

"I won't do that."

"I don't need a keeper."

Without responding, Mara turned around and went back downstairs to find William something to eat. Her hands were shaking as she opened the refrigerator, and she rubbed them together briskly to make them stop while water pooled against her lower eyelids.

Right then and there Mara swore that she wouldn't cry in front of William or let him know how much his dismissal had hurt. He didn't need to deal with her tears in addition to everything else he was facing. She'd fake it like the best of them, and maybe if she pretended to be unaffected, she might start to be able to control herself better.

Mara gave him an hour to become accustomed to the idea that she was there, before heading back up the stairs with a plate of food she had found in the kitchen and warmed up. William had left his bedroom and was in his office, with the phone clutched in his hand, anger written all over his face.

"Here you are," Mara said as she put the plate in front of him before taking one of the bottles of beer out of her other hand, and placing it on the desk. "There's a drink at two o'clock. I don't know about you, but I could use one."

"Mara, you need to go home." William's tone was controlled, yet firm.

"No."

"I've already told Greg to be expecting you. You've seen me, and now I'm asking you to leave. I can take care of myself."

"You're back to that again. I want to make myself perfectly clear. I'm not here to take care of you," she stated with equal determination as she placed silverware next to his plate. Her actions were an obvious contradiction to her statement, but the calm exterior Mara hoped to maintain was intact.

"Then why are you here?"

"You know why." Mara regretted saying that as soon as it came out. To get attention away from the subject, she offered William an exchange. "If you try to eat what I made you, I won't bother you for the rest of the night."

"That's taking care of me, Mara. I'm not an invalid."

"It's justified concern."

"I don't need it."

At a distance closer than Mara had been to him since she arrived, she looked directly at the man who appeared nothing like he had the last time she was in New York.

"Yes you do, Will."

Mara did as she promised by leaving William alone, and other than telling him goodnight after she had unpacked her belongings in a spare bedroom, she made no other contact. Lying awake listening to the sounds in the house, she heard William move about on the second story. The music he played in his office did not drown out the background noise as he went to take a shower, nor did it disguise his pacing up and down the hall.

She also knew when William came to stand outside her door. Despite Mara's prayers that he would knock, he didn't. William simply stood there for several minutes before going into his own room, closing the door behind him, and so ended their first day together.

The second was not much more eventful, with the exception of the heated argument they had in the afternoon, in which Mara announced that she wasn't going to leave unless William came to Vermont with her.

They had butted heads in the past, but it had always been done respectfully. This time, it was an all-out shouting match with no clear winner.

"I don't care if I lose my job, I'm not leaving you!" Mara shouted in the hallway outside his room. They had been able to say about ten sentences to each other before hostilities rose over the subject of her returning home to teach summer school.

"You have to be there on Monday! Stop being so damn stubborn, Mara! I never asked you to come here…"

"I know!" Mara cried out bitterly as the argument then turned personal. "You don't need some insignificant farmgirl in your way. Apparently, I was good enough to sleep with, but when the going got tough, you dumped me like the dead weight you always considered me to be."

"You *know* I never thought of you like that!"

"Bull! That's exactly what happened."

"You're trying to use guilt to force me to do what you want!"

Maybe that was true, but Mara wouldn't budge from her position and neither would he. It was a stormy fight, ending when Mara fled downstairs. William didn't follow after her, and once her footsteps were no longer heard on the stairs, he slammed the door to his room.

Neither spoke to the other for the remainder of the day. They just existed in the same house, with the same sullen expressions on their faces, and without contact. In the months William and Mara had been together, they had never behaved like this toward each other, and their shock at the outburst left them believing that the rift between them was nearing an irreparable stage.

Mara was thoroughly ashamed of herself for using her pain over their breakup like a weapon against William, and sleep that night was not an option. As she sat on her bed trying to come up with a way to make amends for the way she had spoken to him, the simplest solution of them all came to her. Leaving her room, she walked to his bedroom door and knocked lightly.

If William was asleep, she doubted he would hear it, and she would wait until morning to talk to him. Luck was on Mara's side, though, and he acknowledged her right away. Like Mara, William was ashamed of his actions.

"I'm so sorry," Mara said against the wood of the door.

"I am, too."

"May I come in or would you rather I didn't?"

William opening the door was Mara's answer. Taking a step to the side, he invited her into the room they had shared whenever she came to visit him. Mara had always loved the feel of his bedroom, with its masculine colors and heavy woodwork. It had been a sanctuary for them at one time, but now had become a place off limits to her.

"Am I interrupting you?"

"No," William reached out for Mara to take his hand. It was the first time he had touched her since she had arrived. "I was coming to apologize."

"Oh, then I saved you a trip." Letting out a sigh, Mara peered around William. There weren't any lights on, and she could only hope that he hadn't been in the middle of doing something that she might have interrupted. The atmosphere between them was awkward, and Mara was afraid she was going to make another mistake. If only she had known that William was feeling the same way.

Looking down at their hands joined together, she made an attempt to set the situation right. "William, do you think we could manage to talk for a few minutes without getting frustrated or losing our tempers?"

"I know we can."

"Will you sit with me?" The light from the hallway was enough so that Mara could make out an area at the end of the bed where they could sit on the carpet. Settling down, she tugged on William for him to join her.

"Here?"

"Right here." Resting her head against the foot board of William's bed, Mara turned her head to face him while she spoke. "I want to start by saying that I realize I'm making a mess of everything, when all I really wanted you to know is that you have people who care about you. You're not replaceable to us."

Before Mara had come into his room, William had worked out an elaborate apology, which had included explanations about why he had chosen to be alone, but now, as he sat next to her, he was having trouble locating those words.

"I appreciate what you're trying to do."

Still holding hands, Mara rested them over his knee as time passed slowly in the darkness. "I'll be in the classroom on Monday."

The relief that washed over William from her promise showed itself in the small smile that rose to his lips. He had been worried sick about Mara losing her teaching position, and quite possibly any chance she would have of ever teaching again, if she had broken her contract by not showing up.

"But," Mara strongly emphasized the word, "if you asked me to stay, I would."

"I know you would." But William could never ask her to do that. "Mara, do you really believe that I didn't respect you?"

"Sometimes I tell myself that when I need...Sometimes it helps." Mara leaned closer to him. "I can't explain it very well."

"It's not true."

"Thank you." William's confirmation was a both a blessing and a curse. It gave peace to Mara's mind that she had not been imagining what they had between them, but it also took away her greatest defense that she used when her strength ran out, and she just wanted to cry about losing him.

More minutes passed, proving that they could talk to each other calmly and without defenses being raised. William asked her about her family, especially her parents, and Mara described the anniversary party she had helped arrange.

Then Mara took a chance, and in the darkness she whispered to William, "Will you tell me what happened to your sight? All of it?" Without the hesitation she had expected from him, William began his story.

Back in March he noticed that what remained of his vision wasn't as sharp as it had been. Images he had been able to see in the past were becoming nearly impossible to make out, especially when he tried to focus on small objects. At the time, he didn't think that what was occurring would continue, because in the past, the loss had always happened in small increments.

William had himself checked out by his doctor twice after he first recognized the changes, and other than a slight deterioration in the rods and cones related to his known condition, there wasn't any evidence that the other structures of the eyes were affected.

When Mara had been with William on her last visit to New York, different symptoms began to develop. He was seeing bright flashes of light that would come and go, and he had mistakenly judged them as an aftereffect of their going out to a nightclub that had a light show. What was taking place was not a direct symptom of retinitis pigmentosa, although it was in one way related.

In technical terms he explained that his retinas were detaching themselves from the choroids in his eyes. By the time he woke Monday morning the process had completed itself. He went to his doctor immediately, but the blood supply had been cut off for too long. Surgery to reattach them was out of the question as the retinas could not be saved. There was no pain involved.

It wasn't long before William's story ended, as there was no need for him to embellish the facts. After Mara thanked him for telling her, she questioned him no more. Afraid to cross the invisible barrier that separated them as they sat side by side, she kept herself from touching William other than their hands, which were still linked. This went against every instinct screaming inside of Mara to take one more chance by embracing him, risking his rebuff from the contact that she believed was no longer desired or allowed.

Her tender heart was so moved by William's retelling of what he had gone through, that she was finding it impossible not to feel his loss, even though he had delivered his story gently and without emotion.

William had proven himself brave by facing his plight alone, but his move to sequester himself from anyone that might possibly help him was a disservice to the man he was. Mara, Greg, Jane, and his true friends would have been there for him, if he had allowed it, but William's desire for isolation had been stronger than his need to be accepted by them.

Considering that Mara was still very much in love with him, she had done an admirable job of keeping her emotions in check, but the signs that she could no longer hold herself together were bearing down on her. Time was up, and the charade was now over. She needed to get out of the room so William wouldn't witness her breakdown.

"I need to use the bathroom," Mara said quickly as she stood and made her way to the door. She went into the guest bathroom she had always used, closing the door behind her. Turning on the faucet so that the running water would drown out the sounds of her crying, Mara succumbed to her anguish.

The knowledge that William had been by himself when it happened tore her apart. The pain was like a weight on her chest, making it difficult for her to catch her breath whenever she would allow her mind to think about him being suddenly blind and alone.

All the words she couldn't say to William, and the love Mara believed she wasn't entitled to show him came to the surface, and her body shook from the force of her sobs. Sitting on the edge of the bathtub, she held a towel up to her mouth to stifle the noise of her heartbreak, allowing the tears and sorrow to flow freely.

Mara didn't hear the door open, and she didn't hear William say her name as he knelt next to her, encircling her in his arms and bringing her to his chest. His voice was so soft, repeating her name as stroked her hair.

"Don't cry, Mara. I'm not worth it."

"You are to me. How can you say that?" Wrapping her arms even tighter around William, Mara spoke from her heart. "I never would have left you."

"I didn't want you to be with me out of obligation."

"That isn't why I would have stayed." Shaking her head against his chest, Mara didn't open her eyes. It was easier to break the taboo of talking about their relationship in the dark. It also put them on equal footing, since neither could visually confirm the reaction of the other. They had to take each at their word.

"You can't predict what you would have…"

"Yes, I can. William, you've never given me credit for knowing what I'm doing."

"I have."

"No, not when it came to my understanding about your eyes."

It was true, and William knew it. He had sheltered Mara and kept facts from her even though she had proven to him more than once that she was able to comprehend his condition.

"I never meant to hurt you."

"I know that, Will, but you did. Let's be honest with each other. You weren't only concerned about me. You were protecting yourself. You were afraid I wouldn't care about you any more if you were blind."

Again Mara spoke the truth, and William recognized that she was right. He was protecting himself from what he considered the inevitable—losing Mara slowly over time. For a man who championed the blind by raising money for them and donating to their causes, William couldn't see how his life could be just as full as those he was helping. Instead, he lived each day envisioning an imaginary stopwatch over his head, very aware that time itself was running out.

William should have sought out support, but he didn't, relying solely on his own counsel. In his defense, he had been raised in a household where the only person he could go to for guidance was his father, but he was dealing with his own limitations, mild as they were. Therefore, William internalized his fears, and he didn't talk about them to anyone.

Holding Mara as he was right now felt incredibly safe, and taking his lead from her, William also began speaking honestly about what was going on inside of him.

"What if I want to be left alone?"

"That's not you talking. At least not the person I know."

"I don't think he exists anymore, Mara." William was utterly serious, but it was the hopelessness inside of him that was speaking. He was convinced that nothing would ever be the same again, and that the dullness that had taken over his mind would never lift.

"No, you're still in there."

"Look, I sit all day. It takes me hours to motivate myself to get dressed. I've tried, but I can't break free. I'm either angry or I'm numb."

"Then be with people who love you. Come back to Vermont with me."

"I don't want to leave. I have too much to do, too much to get set up. I can't even get to my phone numbers because they were all written down. Nothing in this house was prepared for *this*. I thought I had more time."

"We can take care of that later, after you're back on your feet."

"The doctor gave me these damn pills that don't work."

"They have to build up over time, usually about two weeks. Didn't he tell you about how long it would take to reach a therapeutic level?

"I don't remember. I'm sorry, Mara. I never mean to drag you into this. This is not your problem. I'll be okay."

"Don't be sorry. Come to Vermont, and we can help you while you go through this."

"I don't know."

"Tomorrow's only Saturday. You don't have to decide tonight."

Somewhere between the time that William came in and they started speaking frankly to each other, Mara's tears had ended. Her grief still dwelled within her, but behind it was a force built from understanding. The man she had spent the past two days with had been a stranger, but through his confessions, the William she knew had shown himself.

Without any fantasies that William would begin confessing his love for her and beg her to give him another chance, Mara faced what they did have at the moment. It was a need for each other. Breaking their hold on each other, Mara looked into the eyes of the man she loved. One hundred thoughts ran through her mind, but in the end, what she needed from William wasn't complicated.

"Will, could I sleep next to you tonight?" This wasn't a ploy to become intimate again, but an earnest request made out of loneliness.

Rising to his feet, William reached out for her, and they went back into his room. Lying down together, neither touched the other, although both wished they could hold on tight. Mara could not imagine her life without him in it, and without him still in love with her. They *were* meant to be together, although at the moment they were not.

It was William who made the first move. He asked Mara if she would come closer. What he wanted was to hold her like he did before all of the changes had happened in his life. With her back against his chest, William slid his arm under her pillow and wove the other around her torso. There was comfort for them both in that embrace. It felt so right that without thinking, he ran his lips over her cheek before he said goodnight.

* * *

Mara woke in the morning after the best night's sleep she had in weeks. William's arms were still around her, and she laid still for a moment enjoying the feel of him close to her. She still loved him dearly, possibly even more than before they had broken up, and Mara wasn't ready to give up on him.

What finally prompted her to get out of bed was the personal mission that had been brewing in her mind from the night before. After showering and dressing, Mara returned to William's room where he was still sleeping. The look of determination on her face would have made her father proud.

"Wake up, you," Mara said, gently rubbing his arm to get William to rouse.

"What time is it?"

"You tell me." There was a slight impishness to her voice, as if Mara was challenging him. She waited for him to reach over and touch his clock, letting William find out on his own that it was after nine in the morning.

"It's time to get up." Leaning over to kiss William's forehead, Mara felt rejuvenated, and William was about to become the recipient of her newfound energy. "I'm dressed and heading over to the bakery you took me to last month. I think I'll get us some bagels, unless you want something else."

"No, that's fine." Still groggy, William was hoping that they could go back to sleep for a while.

"That should give you enough time to get showered and start the coffee. I'll meet you downstairs when I get back."

William readily determined that Mara was making him get out of bed because of what he had told her the night before, as she was never very good at being sly. Smiling, mostly for her benefit, he agreed and pushed himself up to a sitting position. Her prodding didn't necessarily make it any easier for William to get out of bed, but it did give him a reason not to waste any more of the morning lying there.

"I'll be back soon." Once Mara walked to the door, an afterthought made her turn around. "William?"

"Yes?"

"You won't lock me out while I'm gone, will you? I really haven't had any coffee yet, and I don't want to be arrested because of all the racket I'll be making at your doorstep without some caffeine in me."

This time, the smile that William gave Mara was real.

"I'll let you back in this once."

When she returned, William was in the kitchen waiting for her with the coffee brewing.

Mara had a full day planned for them, and although no one activity was too taxing, she kept him busy. She had William listen to the news on television and later had him pick out music to play on the stereo. Mara couldn't get William to dance with her, though he was a little tempted when she put on his favorite group, but she tried. And before Mara checked out the voice recognition software Greg had installed on his computer, she opened every window in the house to let fresh air in.

Despite all the diversions she had arranged, Mara didn't believe she was going to cure the depression William was experiencing, but she did one hell of a job getting him to focus elsewhere. Giving the man a break before she approached him about taking a walk outside with her, Mara was cleaning up from lunch when she suddenly let out a string of curse words.

"William!" Mara literally cried as she hobbled into the livingroom where he was. "I need help."

"What's wrong?" Hearing the urgency in her voice, William was immediately on his feet headed toward her.

"I hit my shin hard on the kitchen table. Oh, God, it hurts. I can't straighten my leg out."

"Do you need to go to the hospital?"

"No. I don't think it's broken. It feels more like a surface wound than a broken bone."

"Are you bleeding?" William asked as his hands fell to her side to steady her.

"No, but it burns."

"I'll check it out." Having her lean on him, William guided Mara to the couch before going to his knees on the carpet.

With the lightest touch, William placed his hand on the back of her leg and gently moved his fingers forward to determine the outline of where Mara had injured herself. It was a large area several inches long. Tracing the bone, Mara winced once when the back of his fingers grazed the bottom edge of the bruise, but otherwise the barely perceivable caresses made with his fingertips relaxed her, and soon the muscle in the leg relaxed.

"Heat's coming from your abrasion and there's swelling already, but I don't feel anything out of place. I'd say you're going to have a serious bruise in the morning. I have ice packs in the freezer. Mara, are you sure you don't want to go to the hospital and get it x-rayed?"

"Can we try the ice first?"

"Sure."

William returned with more than ice. Ointment was placed on Mara's scrapped leg before the wound was covered with a large bandage and thin towel to protect it from the cold of the ice pack. They didn't talk while he took care of Mara—she felt foolish, but William was focused. Once everything was cleaned up and put away, he came back to sit down beside her, draping her leg over his lap so he could hold the ice in place.

"Thank you."

Mara's gratitude warmed William's heart, and he realized that he had just taken care of her without regard to his limitations. Her emergency had not been great, but his reactions came naturally, and he had been of use to her. This revelation wouldn't make William suddenly embrace his blindness, but it gave him something to mull over as they sat in comfortable silence while the ibuprofen he had given her began to work.

Mara must have been thinking along the same lines. After she enjoyed his company for a while, and the pain began to dissipate, she turned William into her errand runner for the remainder of the afternoon. She wanted a soda, then the cookies that Gladys had made, and the windows downstairs needed to be shut since it was getting chilly. It soon became a game of Mara making ridiculous requests, and her trying not to laugh when she asked William to do her yet another favor.

"I wish I had my toothbrush," she teased from her position on the couch, trying to make it sound as if her life would be incomplete if her wish went unfulfilled.

"I'm drawing the line there." William smiled to himself, turning his head so she wouldn't see. "I've figured out what you're up to, but you've worn me out."

"So, no toothbrush?" Running her hand over his arm, Mara didn't comment on how much William had done on his own for her that day. He had been all over the house, finding what she needed, and accomplishing what he had set out to do.

"No toothbrush."

"Do you want to know what you could do for me, and this time I'm serious?"

"Name it."

"Would you write more Simon and Iliana for me?"

Iliana was the name of the new character only William had used in his story for Mara, which meant she could only have learned about it from Greg. His hand stopped rubbing the back of her injured leg as he felt self-conscious and excited at the same time.

"Have you read it all?"

"I have. You're an incredible writer."

"Greg explained Christian Moore to you?"

"He did. Don't be angry with him. Greg is one hell of a friend to you."

"I know."

"William, why didn't you tell me about your writing?"

"I was going to explain Christian Moore to you a couple of months ago, but then an idea for a short story came to me. I decided to write it out and tell you that way. Then the story took on a life of its own, and it just kept expanding. Every time I thought I was nearing a point where the story was leveling out, it grew again. Regardless of where I was in the story, I *was* going to give it to you."

"When?"

"On our vacation to Hilton Head this July." The smile faded from William's lips.

Not remarking on their now canceled plans, Mara acted as if the reference didn't exist. "I told Greg it was some of his best work ever, before I knew it was actually you who had written it. That could have been embarrassing, and I'm glad I didn't harp on it."

"Did you like it?"

"Let me tell you how much." That was how they spent their evening—talking, planning, and plotting out his story together. Mara's questions seemed endless, and William enjoyed every moment of it. She spoke as if his continuing the story was a given, as if it would only be a matter of time before he would get back to it. Mara's faith influenced his own.

"I'm going home tomorrow," Mara uttered, as the hour grew late. "I wish I could stay longer. You're probably ready for a break."

"No. I wish you could stay, too."

Mara didn't need to ask William if he were sincere. She could see it. "Greg wants you to come to Vermont. Would you consider it? I'd feel so much better if you weren't here alone."

"I'm not alone. Gladys comes whenever I need her."

"Will, that's being alone."

Mara had a point, and William acknowledged it, but she was asking him to leave behind the place where he felt most secure. It required more than a few minutes of contemplation for him to make a decision. Excusing himself, William rose from the couch.

"I'm going to use the phone and will be right back. Do you need anything while I'm up?"

"No, I'm fine."

While he was gone, Mara heard his telephone ring three times. She didn't know what he was doing or if William was even thinking about her offer, but she didn't allow herself to worry over it. Mara had rediscovered the peace inside of her that had been missing the first two days she had spent in New York. It told her not to push William, even when she believed it was in his best interest, and to give him time to find his own way.

Picking up the glasses and plates from the sofa table, Mara limped to the kitchen. Her leg was going to be fine, and she had been correct that it was not a fracture. Rinsing their dishes and putting them in the dishwasher, Mara kept herself occupied until William came back downstairs.

"I'll go with you tomorrow," William said from the doorway, appearing uncertain of himself.

Why Mara could not savor her victory she didn't know, but William's agreement didn't give her the sense of accomplishment she had believed it would. Instead she thought about the sacrifice he was making by leaving his home.

"Are you going to be okay with this?"

"I think I need to get out of here for a while. I've booked a driver for us. I didn't want to deal with public transportation just yet. Is eleven good for you?"

"It is."

William appeared as if he needed to say more. Walking over to him, she put her arms around his waist while he lowered his lips only inches from her mouth.

"Mara, if I could take back what I told you on the phone that night I called and told you it was over——."

Mara pressed her fingers to William's lips so that he would say no more. She knew she didn't want an apology from him. William's reaction to his loss was not one that could have been dictated, and the concept of right or wrong could not be applied. But she also had to protect herself.

"William, please be very careful what you say to me. I can't cling to false hope when it comes to you."

Heeding her request, William was cautious with what he said next, so that his words would not leave room for misinterpretation.

"I love you."

That night they slept wrapped up in each other, and instead of making love with their bodies, they did so with words. Their minds were at peace knowing that with time and patience, they would both be all right

William and Mara were blessed. If they could remember the lessons they had experienced together during these hard times, it would be doubtful that anything would be able to part them again.

Chapter Six

~~..~~

The week William spent in Vermont passed by quickly. Greg and Jane were gracious hosts, and thankfully, they understood that William didn't require constant companionship to make him feel at home.

Greg learned early on to put things back where he found them, and after an unfortunate incident with a step stool, Jane learned not to leave items in the middle of the room. William knew it had to be difficult for them—the changes to their normal routine that they performed to accommodate him, but it was also made clear to William that they wouldn't have it any other way. And as the days wore on, William began to rediscover parts of his former self.

At times the changes proved too frustrating and William would have to walk away from a situation or else lose his self-control. What he had taken for granted in the past, such as looking up his checking account balance or finding out the weather report, now required several steps to complete, and William was having difficulty adjusting to this.

Greg and William began compiling a list from which they would work, taking each issue as it came and finding solutions to implement so he could maintain his independence. Consultants were then scheduled for the following week to come to William's home in New York to make recommendations and begin installing necessary equipment, programs, and other assistive devices.

Mara continued to be an ever-present force in William's life. She taught during the day, spent her evenings with him, and always returned home at bedtime. They had talked about her spending the night, but both admitted that it didn't feel right to do so with Jane and Greg in the house. They were a little old fashioned in some ways, this being one of them.

Their romantic life remained subdued when compared to how it had been in the past, but their priorities at the moment were focused toward William. The lull in their intimacy was not an area of uncertainty for them, as both were convinced that when the time was right, they would once again become the physical couple they once were. They simply needed to be patient, and take one day at a time.

The pace Mara had been maintaining was beginning to take a toll on her. She went non-stop from six in the morning to nine at night, with her only down time being when she and William would go off by themselves for a few hours each evening. This concerned him, not only because of her health, but for the students she was teaching. They needed her as much as he did, but a reprieve for her was nearing. Next week Mara would have more time to herself, as William was heading back to New York on Sunday with Greg.

William was sitting in a lounger out by the pool when Mara came to Greg's still dressed in the clothes she had worn to school. She bore physical indicators of the stress the past few weeks had had on her, but that was forgotten as a smile lit her face once she located William.

"Hello, you." Mara said as she bent down to kiss him lightly on the mouth.

"How are you today?" William had not been out there to swim, rather to have solitude to think until she arrived.

"Tired." Feeling his hand go around her waist, Mara regretted what she would say next. "I think I'm going to stay for just a little while tonight,"

"Is something wrong?"

"Only the typical summer school fun." Mara answered with a casualness that did not reflect what was truly going on inside of her. She was mentally and physically exhausted, and her day had actually been far from routine. "I'm going to go get a drink of water and be right back."

Listening to her walk away, William could tell that her pace was slower than usual. "Mara, wait! Take mine, and sit next to me for a minute."

After she came back to him, William moved over to make room for her. "Will you tell me about it?"

Mara had become so accustomed to thinking about what William needed that she hesitated sharing her own problems for fear of burdening him. Just as she was about to downplay the events of her day, Mara realized that by doing this she wasn't being fair to William. He didn't ask her to censure her speech based on whether it was pleasant or not, but had asked her how her day went, and that deserved an honest answer.

"Those kids," she began. "They don't care. It's been like pulling teeth to get them to pay attention. They're falling asleep, looking out the window, passing notes. The highlight of my first week happened today. A girl in my class stood up and called me a bitch in front of the other students after I gave her test back."

"What did you do?"

"I marched her down to the office. I know the girl. Her family is bad news, and if she doesn't get her act together, she's going to end up just like them."

"What happened once she was removed from your class? Is she going to be able to make it up next year?"

"She wasn't expelled, William."

"Why not? Students are allowed to curse at teachers now?" William did a remarkable job of conveying a sense of calm.

"I guess so. I was told *indirectly* by our esteemed assistant principal to make certain everyone had an opportunity to pass, and to give her a second chance. This must be a new guideline for Vermont's public schools no one informed me of—to get them through even if they don't learn. You'd be surprised how many of those kids have trouble reading."

"That was the action taken?"

"No, she was given after school detention and instructions to write me a letter apologizing for her outburst. It's days like this when I think that I could have been working in some nice, clean drugstore dispensing medications and drawing about three times the pay."

"You wouldn't have been bored doing that?" William took her hand in his own, knowing she was not one to balk from a challenge.

"I probably would have."

"Do you like teaching?" William had asked her this question before, but today was the first time Mara had brought up what she could have been doing if she had been able to finish pharmacy school.

"Not today, but yes, I do. I think I'm cut out for it."

William turned his attention back to Mara's problem. "You said the kids weren't paying attention. What do the students in your class *need* to know?"

"If I could teach them what I have in my notes, I'd feel good about it. I want them to be exposed to the basics."

"Are you covering more than that right now?"

"Yes. We're following the book."

"What if you just covered what was in your notes?" William's interest was sincere. "Would that be enough?"

"I don't know. I'll have to think on it."

Quietness came over them as Mara rested her head against his shoulder. The relationship they had been rebuilding since she had come to New York could not be repaired with a simple kiss. It went deeper than that into the realm of trust, but their love for each other was genuine, and this was what would help them along.

"Your dad stopped by again this afternoon." Grinning, William turned his face toward her. "He talked to me about his cows."

"He likes you," Mara chuckled. Her father had been out to Greg's every day since William came to Vermont, and the fondness Mara claimed to be her father's was real.

"I like him, too. Will you let me take you out tonight?"

Mara's response of laughing out loud was not exactly the response William had expected. "Oh Lord. I thought you said something about making out tonight. My mind is in the gutter!"

"That's a healthy place for it to be." William replied enthusiastically.

"Spoken like a man! Now, what did you say?"

"Do you want to go out tonight?"

Mara wondered if William meant out to her house, or out on a date. If it were the latter, this would be his first venture into public with the exception of the doctor appointments he had been to, and to her that was a sign that William was becoming more confident with himself. Either way, she would get some much-desired time alone with him.

"How about just dinner since you're tired?" William asked before she was able to give him an answer.

"That sounds nice."

"I'll get changed. Will you let Greg know where we're going?" Standing up, William reached out to help Mara to her feet.

"I will, but I don't know where we're going."

"Anywhere you want, but I'd prefer somewhere not too populated."

Thinking for a minute, Mara laced her fingers with his as they headed toward the house. "I know the perfect place. How do cheeseburgers sound to you?"

Mara took William to a bar and grill off of an old county road in the middle of nowhere that was twenty minutes from where she lived. Only locals frequented the place, with its aged interior and makeshift stage for regional bands that would play on the weekends. It was too early in the evening for there to be many people inside, which she preferred since Mara planned on talking William through the building as he used his cane.

Not a stumble or misstep was had before they sat in a booth across from each other. Mara read the menu for William and told him what she wanted so he could order for the both of them. This had always been a custom of his, taught to William by his father as a way to show respect toward a lady, and though it was an outdated practice, Mara found it charming.

"I'm going to miss you next week." She said after the waitress had taken their order and delivered their sodas.

"Do you want to come for the weekend? Or I could come back here?" He shared Mara's sentiment. In some ways William felt closer to her now, and he wondered if it was because she had seen him at his absolute lowest and still remained by his side.

"I'd like to go there to see what you and Greg are going to have done. I can take the train next weekend."

William began telling her about the Braille tutor he had lined up when they were interrupted. A man, dressed in a police officer's uniform came over to their booth, but he wasn't there on official business.

"Mara?" The man asked amiably. The smile on his face was friendly, and a little wary.

"Hi Jeff. How are you?" She returned equally as friendly.

"Good. And you?"

"Doing great. Jeff Kennedy, this is William Grant."

Jeff extended his hand for William to shake, but it was not expected and therefore ignored. Before Jeff could withdraw his hand, Mara gave him a sign to wait and whispered to William 'handshake.'

"I'm sorry. It's good to meet you." To his credit, Jeff immediately understood that William was blind, and there was no harm done by the oversight. Insignificant small talk was then made and it was not long before Jeff excused himself after asking Mara to give her parent's his regard.

"That was a nice man," William commented after he was certain Jeff was out of earshot.

"You sound like Greg," Mara teased. "Yes, he is."

"He likes you."

"You're wrong, William. We went out for a while last year, but it was nothing more than that. He's a state policeman."

"What happened?"

"I don't know. It just fizzled out. There's nothing wrong with Jeff, but it just wasn't *there*, if you know what I mean."

"Explain 'there'." William teased back, acting as if he didn't comprehend Mara's meaning of the word.

"You know what *there* is. Like when you're talking to someone on the phone and you hang up, only to call back later with some pathetic excuse just because you wanted to hear their voice again. Or you daydream about their hands on you at the most inappropriate times, and you don't feel guilty about it. Things like that."

"So it wasn't there with Jeff?"

"Oh, no. I have the hots for another guy, anyway. He's sexy, and intelligent, kind, and he writes stories for me." Mara leaned over the table and kissed him. "I love him."

She was about to retake her seat when William pulled Mara closer, kissing her a second time. "He's very lucky. I'd bet that he loves you, too."

Moving so her lips were close to his ear, Mara hesitated before she responded. William's good mood was contagious, and she didn't want to put a damper on the evening by changing their plans, but she was missing him in ways that kissing and holding hands wouldn't replace.

"Will you spend the night with me? I know we're taking things slow, and I don't—." Sighing, Mara tried to lighten her request by returning to the teasing they had been engaging in. "You can call Greg and tell him that I kidnapped you."

"God, yes." William answered seriously. Mara wasn't the only one missing their closeness. "Do you think it's too late for the cook to box up our food?"

Glancing over at the grill, Mara could see that their order was still cooking. "No."

"Let's take it with us."

At the end of July, William and Mara traveled together to South Carolina to Hilton Head Island. He had come so far during the nearly two months since he had lost his vision. This trip, which had been planned long before, was their gift to each other.

As the pre-morning breeze rushed past her to enter the house, Mara stood alone at the screen door in the stillness. White linen curtains in the livingroom danced to a rhythm conjured up by the sea. They could not excite her concentration from her search of the darkness as it followed the light from the porch until it illuminated the sole figure of a man.

He had a ritual he performed religiously since they arrived—to go out before the dawn and sit on the beach as the sun made its appearance. William told her it was a habit he had acquired when he was young, but Mara believed it to be more. He was always peaceful when he returned, and some of their most revealing conversations had occurred afterward as they held warm coffee mugs in their hands.

The healing properties of water have long been written about, but until she came to Hilton Head Island, Mara didn't give any credence to the claims. There was no tangible evidence to support such statements, but now that she had been here with William, she was a believer. Physically they were both as they should be, but this was not where nature's salve needed to be applied.

Mara mustn't have been looking when William stole the last bit of her heart, but it most assuredly had occurred during this week at the beach house. Unaccustomed to the feeling of defenselessness, Mara's emotions went back and forth between joy and trepidation. There was nothing she could do. Mara was completely in love.

Taking a cotton blanket from the back of a chair, she stepped outside to join him.

"Good morning," William said as he heard her approach. "The tide's beginning to come in."

"It's chilly, so I brought a wrap. May I sit with you?"

He couldn't see her smile, but William knew it just the same. His arm reached out in place of a verbal response and she grasped it, guiding herself to sit between his legs. The blanket was handed to William, which he unfolded and placed around the both of them while Mara settled up against his chest. Cool cotton pressed against her back, the nightgown she wore not offering protection against the chill. Soon the cover trapped the heat from their bodies and a comfortable warmth built.

Closing her eyes, Mara began to understand what was going on around her. The longer she used her sense of hearing for orientation, the more she was able to distinguish. With each minute that drifted by, she relaxed more in the security of William's body encircling hers. He didn't flinch when a noise startled her, nor did he seem concerned with the sounds she could not identify.

There is a natural vibration that comes from the sea as it moves inland, low and nearly unperceivable if one does not seek it out. Mara experienced this marvel for the first time while on the beach of Hilton Head.

"What are you doing?" William asked as his mouth skimmed her bare neck.

"I'm listening." With her eyes remaining shut, Mara replied softly, not wishing to disturb the phenomena surrounding them. Time passed, and they did not move except for William drawing her nearer.

"I wish we could make this last forever." Mara's head fell back to rest on his shoulder, her statement whispered as if he had it in his power to do so. William actually did have the power to ensure they would never have to leave, but it was an unrealistic way to live. Edens were best appreciated when balanced with real life to give them meaning.

"How do people stay in love?" Mara's fears were coming out to play in the darkness and expressing them hadn't been planned. She was not a dramatic woman who used words and actions to create an illusion of someone she could never be. The words she chose seemed alien to her as they slipped through her lips because they were not forthright but concealed her insecurity. Mara and William held on to one another. *Time* eluded them but held the answers to their questions.

"I don't know. I think it's their priorities that make a difference." Fingertips roughened by countless hours of writing traveled the narrow ridge of her chin. William couldn't account for it, but his hands rarely strayed from her. The occasional touch gave him reassurance that Mara was there, in much the same way as she would gaze across the room at him. Both served the same purpose.

William brought the blanket closer around them, and without notice, an hour slipped by. Mara only opened her eyelids twice during that period. Once to answer a question of William's and the other to make certain a nearby bird was not too close to them.

"May I say something I'm not sure you'll want to hear?" William nodded, granting her permission to voice whatever she needed. "You have the most stunning eyes I've ever seen on a man—huge and brown. They're animated and you use them when you talk...even still. I believe they're one of your finest features."

Mara's words made love to an attribute that William had grown to despise. He never acknowledged any value in his eyes since they had failed him so completely, yet this woman looked past their uselessness to find virtue where he had only given scorn. What Mara said did not change William's opinion, as it had been too many years in the making, but it did for a moment give him an opportunity to view himself differently.

Feeling the rays of light upon his face as the sun began to rise, William stood and helped Mara to her feet, dusting the sand loose from their clothes. Hand in hand they walked back to the house, the blanket draped around her shoulders. Wondering if she had offended him since William said nothing, Mara intended to clear the air over their morning coffee.

Once inside and certain they were safely away from the prying eyes of strangers, he walked her backward until she was flush with the door. Pressing his bodyweight against her with forearms leaning on the door, William's mouth sought out Mara's. A fine dusting of salt from the sea spray burned a small cut he had on his lower lip, the sensation easily overlooked when compared to the choice of tasting her.

Mara's habit of voicing opinions that shook him to his core was something that William would never become accustomed to, but he lived for them.

"The last time I saw you clearly was when you were getting into a taxi, smiling at me as you said good bye. You were beautiful." William's voice trailed off as the images sprang to life. "I can see it as plainly as if it was happening now. Your image will not change in my mind. Say you love me."

"I love you," she complied as her nails dug into his hair.

What had started out with gentle intentions instantaneously combusted into a passion derived from need. Need for reassurance, the need to be wanted, and the need to know that this was real and not a dream derived from a lonely mind summoning fantasy.

Her nightgown soon slipped from her shoulders without much effort and fell to her feet. The heat from his hands, as they burned a trail across her body, alternated with the cool breeze now swirling in the room. This wasn't the first time they had spontaneously lost themselves to the urges of their bodies, but as they had become more familiar over time, the sex intensified.

Going to his knees after she had removed his clothes, William ran his hand over the area between her legs before lifting his mouth close to her breast. "Mara—," was all the warning he gave before two fingers slipped inside of her, palm out, to stroke the sensitive area of her upper wall that he had found months ago. That was when William noticed something out of the ordinary—what he felt on his fingers as he moved them within her was his semen from the night before. The idea of Mara carrying remnants of their lovemaking within her brought a rush of blood between his legs.

"Oh God," he groaned. This would not be a repeat of the night before when they made gentle love. Instead it would mimic the recklessness occurring outside their refuge, as the tide intensified, crashing inland with a force constant and unbreakable.

Mara's hips pivoted outward to accommodate him as her hands held William's head to her breast. The distinction between pain and pleasure faded when her senses became overloaded. It split her concentration until they finally melded into one rhythm.

"I'm close." Mara said, and his efforts increased, bringing about an intensity that in turn created the most exquisite, indescribable pleasure.

It was shattering when it hit. The peak began with a ripple effect as contractions came in rapid succession with no pause, one after the other, almost tumbling over themselves to be expelled. The stronger ones lasted longer, yet time in this instance was counted in half-seconds. Just as they slowed, William once again coaxed them to continue by engaging the area with a lighter touch.

They had done their homework and practice *does* make perfect. Pulling her forward so that she was on her hands and knees, they both knew this position would prolong her pleasure, as the angle of his penetration would press on the awakened spot.

"Lose yourself." A ragged directive came from Mara's throat. Chills broke out down her arms after she said those words, announcing a fresh wave of orgasm, needing just a little more incentive to break. "Don't hold back, Will."

William pushed into the opening that stretched to admit him, the depth inside soft and engorged, enveloping the length of his member. Mara's moans and broken sentences increased in volume as a tempo established itself.

With his hands gripping her hips, William brought her down firmly on himself. Each stroke drew him closer to the end, but an end that held the promise of flooding her with ecstasy. This woman was made for him.

Just as his own crest neared, Mara's began again. The undertow between contractions pulled William farther inside, hitting hard and deep. It was the turning point for him, and with a violent shudder, William released inside of the woman who owned his heart.

When it was over, William lowered his cheek against Mara's bare back. "I love you," he whispered upon her skin.

"I know."

Epilogue

The Months Turned
Into a Year…

~~..~~

Mara read the nameplate on the door before slipping into the refuge of the woman's bathroom off of the teacher's lounge. Nodding at the only other person she could see, Mara ducked into a stall and closed the door behind her before fumbling for her cell phone in her book bag. Dialing the number, she waited until she heard the other woman exit before sending the call to home.

"I have to talk fast before anyone else comes in." She said once she heard William pick up.

"What's up?"

"These students…they're sophisticated! I don't know, Will. I might have made a mistake"

"They're a pack of kids."

"Kids carrying six hundred dollar purses and looking at me like I'm going to be on the lunch menu next week." Mara was not faking her anxiety, but thankfully William knew what to do. He challenged her.

"Science girl is afraid of the unenlightened? I find that hard to believe." He replied in a sarcastic tone.

"Hum...unenlightened, you say?"

"Who's your hero?" William bit down on his lip so he would not laugh.

"Marie Curie! Nobel Prize winner in chemistry and physics. I know her biography by heart."

"Where are the answers to all of life's questions?"

"In science." Mara answered back sharply.

"What do interesting people talk about at a dinner party?"

"That's an easy one. Science."

"What is the one subject people misinterpret more than any other?"

Raising her free hand in the air, Mara answered. "Science."

"What's your mission in life?"

"To set them straight." William's teasing had worked and Mara settled down. After explaining that she was having a bad case of first day of class jitters, she made a request of him. "Put Ralph on the phone."

"Ralph," William called out. This was not the first time Mara had asked him to do this. "Ralph, you have a phone call."

Into the room trotted a German Shepherd, his heavy frame imitating the sound of thunder when his paws hit the wood floor. He was an intimidating mass of one-year-old flesh, and they had some legitimate concerns about his fitting in Mara's car if he grew anymore. If Ralph had not had his tail wagging while his tongue was hanging out of his mouth, he might even be considered frightening.

"Sit." William said to his Seeing Eye dog, putting the phone up to his ear once he had obeyed. "Here's Ralph."

"Hello, sweet baby." Mara cooed. "How is my boy today? Do you miss me? You're the best dog in the entire world and I love you. Are you being treated well? I'll tell William to give you an extra steak bone because you are so good—."

William waited patiently until Ralph barked, a sign that Mara had told him to do it, before getting back on the phone.

"Will, don't forget to take the trash out today. Okay?"

"You whisper sweet nothings to the dog," William said dryly. "Then remind me to do a filthy chore?"

Mara let out a belly laugh. She loved it when William played the part of the abused husband, even if they had only been married for two months. "Put Peaches on the phone, sweetie."

"I can't. She's in Purgatory."

"Did she pee on the floor again?"

"I heard it right after I brought her in from outside." A genuine smile danced across his lips. "We'll be there at four this afternoon to walk you home from school."

"Thank you." The warning bell announcing the first period sounded in the room. "I have to go. You know I'm thinking about you today."

"I need to stay busy." William admitted.

"You haven't read any papers, yet?" All of their papers came in both print and Braille, which William was quite good at reading.

"I'm going to let Greg read them first."

"I was *so* tempted this morning to peek when the Times arrived."

"Go to class." William laughed. "You're making me nervous."

"Why don't you work on housetraining Peaches to pass the time? It will take all day and you'll get nowhere." Mara exited the stall she had been hiding in. "I have to hang up now. I love you."

"I love you, too. You'll do fine."

Once Mara made it to her classroom, she took a moment to look at the faces of the students in her class. She thought about how young they looked as she unbuttoned her lab coat and took it off. It was too warm for the extra clothing, and underneath the jacket she wore her 'Science Rocks' tee shirt a former student had made for her.

Many raised eyebrows and snickers echoed through the room, but there was one boy sitting in the front row who looked at her with an expression of understanding. Meeting his gaze, Mara gave him a small smile as a shared appreciation passed between them. Then she started her class.

"Hello. I'm Mrs. Grant and this is chemistry one. If you're not *supposed* to be in chemistry, now might be a good time to leave the room. For those staying, please put your book under your seat. You won't need to bring it with you to class, unless I tell you to beforehand. *I'll* be teaching you the basics of chemistry—."

Two life altering events were happening on this day for William and Mara. Hers was that she was not starting the first day of class in Vermont, but in New York City five blocks from where she and William lived.

William had heard about the job opening in January, and knowing that Mara had already applied for her teaching license in the state of New York, it was almost too good to be true that a school within walking distance was needed a chemistry teacher for the following school year.

Because the school was in a good location, the competition was going to be stiff. Mara believed she had little hope of getting the position, but with ongoing encouragement from William she went into the interview with the attitude that she already had the job. Before she arrived there was a rumor floating among the board members that she was engaged to William Grant, a man known for his philanthropic endeavors.

When Mara interviewed, dollar signs were already in the eyes of some of the board members as they thought about what William could help do for the school. But this is not what got her the job in the end. It was her enthusiasm that won them over and earned her the position.

Mara received confirmation that she was hired in May. In June, she and William married on Hilton Head Island at the house his family owned. The ceremony was small with only close relatives in attendance, and Ralph of course.

Ralph especially liked the morning ritual he and William shared while they were in South Carolina. At sunrise man and beast would go out onto the beach, and William would toss a ball into the tide for Ralph to retrieve.

Mara and William spent their entire three-week honeymoon there. Four days before they were to return home to New York, he and Ralph came back late one morning with a female German Shepherd puppy tucked under William's arm as a gift for Mara.

William had met a man on the beach shortly after they were married, and noting that Ralph was a Seeing Eye dog, the man mentioned that he knew of puppies for sale by a woman who trained them.

It was difficult to do, but William was able to be secretive enough to get a hold of the breeder only to find out there was one pup left. She did not think the puppy would make a good trained animal, but the dog's temperament would make an excellent pet.

Mara was sitting on the front porch eating a peach when William put the restless puppy down. It was love at first sight for Mara. She called her over, the pup stole the peach from her hand and took off running into the house. She had been wreaking havoc ever since. This is how Peaches got her name.

Before they were married it was agreed between them that because of William's continued work as a fundraiser, New York was where they needed to live. They could have stayed in Vermont since his work peaked during the autumn and winter months, but the traveling back and forth was needlessly stressful on all of them.

William subsequently purchased the house in the country Mara rented from her uncle, so they would have a place of their own to come to when they were able.

William continued to write. The year between his losing his sight and their marriage he took the text he had authored for Mara and expanded it into a four hundred-page book. Two trips to the editor later, Christian Moore was starting a new series where Simon and Iliana were the lead characters.

Greg approved of the direction of the new plot and went through his friend's manuscript changing words here and there, so that no one except the most astute fan would be able to tell that someone else wrote it. Both men maintained their ability to remain anonymous.

At the same time that Mara started her first day as a New York City public school teacher, the reviews on William's book were due to come out in the papers and online. They made a pact that William would not find out what the reviewers wrote in the various publications until after Mara was at school, due to her anxiousness on both accounts.

They had a lot riding on how the story was received. If all went well, William was going to take over Greg's role as the writer, giving

Greg the opportunity to start writing a group of stories completely unrelated to their vampires and under a new name. If the reviewers did not approve of William's first attempt then the two men would finish out their contract with their publisher working in the roles they had before.

William was outside the school at four as he told Mara he would be. Ralph stood harnessed by his side and Peaches was at his feet wrapping her leash around his legs. A few brave students had stopped to pet the dogs while William waited, most of the attention going to the puppy as Ralph stood guard next to his owner.

"You're smiling." Mara said after she took Peaches's leash and kissed him.

"I am."

"It's a big smile, William. Is it because you're glad to see me?"

"Partially. How was your day?"

"The students think I'm crazy, so it was fine. Tell me!"

William leaned down and lowered his voice. "Do you want to wait until we get home?"

"No."

"It's all good, Mara."

"All good? Even from that ass critic you've always despised?"

"Yes!" William's smile broadened. "His biggest complaint was that it was too short."

"It was four hundred and seven pages!"

"There's more. He admitted in his column that he was prepared to hate the story because he never did like Simon, but by the end of the first chapter he was starting to change his mind."

"What did Eve say?" Eve was Christian Moore's publisher, and her word was like that of God.

"She said that if it sells as well as she expects, she wants to know when I can get the next one done. Greg has called seven times already today. I think he was weeping after he talked to Eve, mumbling something about mysteries based on psychic CIA detectives…I have no idea what he was talking about."

"I am so damn proud of you!" Mara hugged him, kissing William over and over. They were such a team—each other's strongest supporter. Where Mara was lacking, William thrived, and her strengths helped to make up for his weaknesses. They *were* meant to be together. "We have to celebrate!"

"I've already ordered food in for tonight. Greg and Jane are coming this weekend, and we'll all go out…" With her arm around his waist they started to head for home while talking a mile a minute to each other. Mara could hardly wait to read the reviews, knowing that the critics were going to see in William what she, Greg, and Eve already knew.

At the first crosswalk a phenomenon occurred that could have been considered a sign of more good things to come.

"William, Peaches stopped at the curb." Mara whispered to him so she would not startle the dog. "I think she's following Ralph's lead."

"There may be hope for her yet. Although, I'm getting accustomed to her chaotic ways."

"I know. She's not subdued like me at all." William laughed at Mara's blatant lie as the light changed. "I have to make a confession because it's eating away at me. Do you want to hear it?"

"Yes."

"I slept with Christian Moore last night."

"Was he any good?" Damn if Mara saying that didn't give William the chills.

"Oh, yes. We did it in the shower."

"Stop." William, Mara, and Ralph all stopped once they had crossed the street. Peaches let out a small yelp when she ran out of leash because she had kept on walking. In his sexy tone, William made Mara a promise. "When I get you home—."

~~ The End ~~

Bonus Short Story

~~..~~

The Dreams of Michelangelo

~~..~~

University of Dallas.
Irving, Texas.

The Spring Gala was well underway and judging from the turn
out, this year's exhibition would be more heavily attended than the
last. Eager and curious students packed the auditorium for a chance
to view their instructor's creative abilities during this annual open
house, but the real excitement would begin at midnight when each
piece's master would be revealed. Until then speculation buzzed
about the room as to which man or woman went with the different
displays. A few were easy to guess. Tim Kerr only worked in metal,
therefore the one metal sculpture in the room surely belonged to him.
But others were more difficult to identify.

Mark Olson stood in front of an oversized mural done in oil not
really caring which colleague had painted it at the moment. It was the
picture itself that held his attention. Originally he believed the long
flowing lines of the paintbrush blending the different hues into one
was what made the work interesting, but the longer he gazed at it, the
more he realized this was not the cause. Anyone could mimic the
technique; it wasn't that uncommon or difficult to perform.

The scene was vaguely unique. A young woman clothed in a sheer white muslin gown lying on a boulder located on a natural shoreline. The arch of her body molded to the rock and her arms were over her head with fingers dug deep into the sand. He had seen this particular pose numerous times in the past, although the tilt of her head did lend it a fresher look. Refusing to be too critical of the painting, he moved closer to it.

Mark Olson's true weakness in personality came through in regard to his own art. In this area he became the Mr. Hyde of the famous duo, and his patience was often lost to the moment. He couldn't tolerate distraction when the mood hit, and to break from the creative process for any reason could send him into angry raptures. It was this state of hyper-focus in which some of Mark's best work was actualized, yet the man who was one part beloved teacher occasionally gave way to the plagued sculptor.

Often his models left him in a fit of tears after hours of excruciating pain and fatigue, swearing never to sit for him again. Obsession was the cross he bared when working in his preferred medium of stone and tools, and he did not realize the passing of time or need of others during inspiration.

It was not in Mark's nature to be callous, but this was how he was interpreted time and time again.

Allowing his eyes to rest on the face of the model in the mural, Mark's mind wondered if it was the woman who made the painting fascinating and not the artist at all. While he was considering the possibility, a person came up and stood beside him. Without looking, Mark knew who it was, and his body involuntarily stiffened with the knowledge his intuition supplied.

Sandy blond hair worn at the stage where it needed a trim lay neatly against the head of the man next to Mark, giving the false impression that he was approachable. Underneath the handsome exterior of Joel Foster was the true man, neither humane nor sympathetic toward the other blessed individuals he was to share the world with. The chief concern in Joel Foster's little universe was Joel Foster, and to hell with anyone who invaded his space without permission. He had not the time nor effort to waste on the uninvited.

For reasons only God and Foster understood, Mark Olson was one of the minority that Foster needed approval from. He never gave any outward indication that this need was real for him, in fact, he took the approach of acting out the opposite. Foster would make his verbal jabs at Mark on occasion, to prove his dominance and superiority, but they always fell for naught. Mark was not impressed, and his manner often reflected the lack of consequence he had for the man.

The only reason Mark had any contact with him was because he was Foster's teaching assistant for one of his classes. The pay justified the annoyance, and Mark truly enjoyed that aspect of the university life.

Unable to remain silent, Foster stepped back from the portrait to show that he was ready for conversation on the piece.

"Tell me your impression, Mark. You seem enamored. Is it the artist you are tying to distinguish or something more? The use of colors, perhaps?"

Mark realized that Foster was talking down to him like a teacher to a student, and outside of the classroom he had little patience for this type of behavior. If it weren't for his need for good will from Foster when it came time to evaluate his performance as a teaching assistant, he would have walked away without comment.

"It is neither." He commented dryly, not moving his gaze from the painting.

"Oh? Don't be at a loss for words. Speak your mind."

Mark turned his head to look directly at Foster. The curtness in his tone would not be missed.

"Do you want a technical evaluation or a personal interpretation?"

"Personal will do. I know how you sculptors describe paint, and I'd rather not hear how 'chiselable' her face is."

"Personally," Mark began, turning back to the portrait, "I think it's the way the artist captured the girl that makes the painting. There's something almost virtuous about her, yet she doesn't appear to be purely innocent. Look at how her skin captures the light. It's like an aura, and possibly this is what gives off the illusion of innocence. I'll admit that I'm having trouble pinpointing the right words to characterize the feel of the painting."

Mark stepped closer to the display, and without desiring a reply from Foster, he continued.

"Do you notice how softly the painter did the breasts and hips? This leads me to believe that a woman might have been the artist." Foster twitched after Mark's comment. "They weren't exaggerated to show sexuality like most men tend to do, but left natural and unobtrusive. I almost believe that the model could have been a man on the rock, and it wouldn't have made a difference. It is more the feel the woman gives off, as opposed to her sexuality, that is interesting."

"So, you believe that only a woman could have presented this girl in a more asexual light?" Foster asked, his voice clipped with hostility.

"No, those weren't my exact words. I believe that a woman can have more appreciation for the model herself, and often doesn't dwell on proving her subject's womanhood as much as a man might." With his index finger, Mark made circles in the air around the subject's face. "The face is the key. I can see peace in it underneath the discomfort that she is trying to disguise."

"Discomfort? I don't see any discomfort."

"Look closer. It's hidden in the neck muscles. See how they stand out?"

"Hum—." Foster grunted.

"Something I would like to know is if the artist painted the girl true or if they added the persona to the actual person? Is there a woman who can emit this sort of…" Mark raised his hands to show that he was without words.

"So, are you telling me that from this painting you only walk away with wanting the girl's phone number? It does nothing else for you?" Foster sounded almost exasperated.

"No," a deep frown creased Mark's forehead. "No. That was not my point."

"Then you like the painting?"

"Like? That's not the right word. Admire or appreciate is closer. I'm not saying that the artist was overly original in their presentation, but the girl completes the painting…or maybe I should say how the artist interpreted the girl is what makes the painting."

Foster nodded his head. "You would give this artwork a positive rating?"

"Definitely."

"Thank you."

The tone Foster used told Mark he was standing next to the man who painted the picture. Joel Foster. For a moment the piece lost its luster as he placed the man he despised with the painting he favored, but Mark fought not to allow the scorn he felt for Foster's previous work to cloud his appraisal. Silence reigned for some time before Mark broke it with a question.

"Who is she?"

Once again they were on the subject of the model, and this is not what Foster wanted to discuss. He was standing there for more praise, not to talk about some girl he hired to sit for him.

"Still wanting a date, I see." Malice laced his remark, and Mark would not justify Foster with an answer.

"She's just some student here. I called up employment and picked her out from a large group of other non-descript people. There really isn't anything special about her. Quite dull, if you ask me, and she could stand to lose a few pounds."

Foster was lying through his teeth. The model was actually booked by him for the next two months for more sittings. There was something about the girl that brought out his best work in years. Of course, for Foster to admit this would be for him to concede that he needed the inspiration, and this was not the impression he wished to give.

"Were you able to capture her true or did you embellish?" Mark knew how to phrase his question to get an honest answer out of Foster.

"True," was said under his breath. "That is exactly how she looked on the rock. The landscape is false, but the girl is real."

"Very interesting." Mark's eyes locked with the woman's. "What is her name?"

"Ah...my little secret." He smiled smugly.

"She doesn't want to be known?"

"I don't discuss my models."

This caught Mark's attention since it was an outright lie. He had heard Foster on several occasions give out personal information about the men and women that posed for him. Taking a moment to try to understand why Foster would claim such a falsehood, Mark decided that it wasn't worth wasting time on and prepared to move away.

Sensing his loss of interest, Foster spoke up quickly. "I saw your display at the table. It is...good."

To be more correct, it was better than good. Mark had bought a large stone at a nearby nursery and carved out the face of a man into it. Using plaster, he filled the forged cavity to check the accurateness of the image, cautiously making the final cuts with his chisel until it was perfect. He named the work Dire Consequence due to the painful, distorted expression he had given it. To date Mark thought of it as one of the best in his collection.

Foster's "good" meant nothing to him, and with a nod of the head he left the man. For the rest of the evening Mark was unaware that a pair of watchful eyes followed him wherever he went.

For a man as exhausted as he was when he went to bed, Mark tossed and turned unable to achieve restful sleep. Jumbled in his dreams were scenes from the gala he had left not an hour ago. Some of the conversation was warped and twisted in pieces, leaving him confused and agitated. In this state of chaos he made his way through the crowd and over to the only area in the room that wasn't shoulder-to-shoulder people—in front of the painting of Her.

Blocking out the dream noise behind him, Mark studied the portrait with hidden enthusiasm. He would attempt to study the background or features other than her, but his eyes always found their way back to the woman. The pose Foster had put her in was supposed to be sensual, but it wasn't...yet it was.

Difficult to explain, it was as if Mark could *see* that she was not feeling sensual while she sat for Foster, and that in itself was what made him so attracted to the painting. It was like they shared a secret.

Finally giving up on trying not to focus on her, he stared at her with wonder as the changes that took place before him were so slow in developing that he missed the first few. It was her hand coming up from the sand that he noticed. Startled, Mark backed a half step away and watched with wide eyes as the woman in the painting came to life.

"It's only oil." He told himself. "It's not real or breathing, but oil."

The woman in the painting cocked her head as she took her turn studying him. After stretching her arms over her head, she stood and offered him a hand.

"Join me?" Her voice was feminine and light, but without any other distinguishing characteristics.

Mark only stared in response. He knew he was dreaming, therefore her offer was not a complete surprise to him, but to be able to join her? He couldn't comprehend what she meant by her invitation.

"Close your eyes." She instructed him confidently. "I will show you how."

He did what she suggested.

"Now, open them and you will be here." It was the words she spoke that planted the possibility in Mark's mind, and as she had said, when he opened his eyes he was standing next to her in the painting.

"It was too easy," he told himself as he reached over and touched the still warm boulder she was lying on. Confused, Mark bent down and scooped up a handful of sand, letting it sift through his fingers. He could feel the grains against his skin, and again he reminded himself that what he was experiencing was not real.

"You do not seem pleased. Do you find me unattractive, strange, an anomaly?"

"No. You are beautiful to me."

He took a few steps to stand closer to the fathom from the painting. By some natural substance her swollen lips looked as if they were colored, but they were not. Mark could barely tear his eyes away from them as he brushed the sand off his hands.

"Do want to kiss me?" The woman smiled slightly in her own amusement, but Mark remained serious.

"Yes." He mouthed.

"Why?"

"I don't know." He took another step toward her. "Where did you come from?"

"The painting."

"No...I mean where can I find you? In real life?"

She shook her head. "You must seek me out on your own. That which is most worth having is often the most difficult to obtain. Is that not true?"

"It is," he answered.

"Then don't let the grass grow under your feet, or I may be gone."

"Give me an idea as to where to start the search." Reaching out he was able to take hold of her hand. Feeling warm solidness pressed against his palm, Mark looked down at her.

"I can touch you!" There was a childlike wonder in his voice.

"I thought you said I was only oil?" A mischievous raise of an eyebrow exposed a playful manner, once again encouraging Mark to take the final step forward that was separating them.

Running his eyes over her entire body, the rhythmic rise of her shoulder alerted him to the fact that she was breathing. Bringing the hand up that he still was holding, he placed her wrist against his lips and felt for a pulse.

"You're alive," Mark uttered against the skin, "I can feel blood rushing through your veins."

An inviting smile was issued in his direction, and Mark caught sight of it out of the corner of his eye.

"Come sit for me in my studio?" His request was his true desire. She didn't answer.

"Let me recreate you in stone," he placed her arms around his neck and her fingers went to hide in the depth of his dark hair.

"...And clay," his hand brushed down her back, stroking the flesh under the thin material she wore.

"...And charcoal." The sensations building inside of him were becoming painful as he thought about possessing her.

"I can't leave the picture." Tilting her chin up to look upon his face, the woman gently brought his head down until they were mere inches apart. "Could you stay?"

"I can stay," Mark agreed. He stared into her eyes intensely for some time before asking her the question he had yet to find an answer to. "What is it about you?"

"You'll have to figure that out yourself. I will not tell you your own motivation."

"I just want to crawl up inside of you and..." his mouth came down hard on hers, yet he continued to speak. "Can I touch you more?"

"Like an artist or a man?"

"Both" burst forward from his throat.

"Mark..." the woman began to passionately kiss him back, matching his need with an imaginary force of her own. His head began to sway as his body responded to the movement of her lips.

She was the one who broke the contact between their mouths, and with one hand pressed against his chest, she guided him backwards to sit on the rock.

Mark's hands roamed freely over her, fingertips memorizing her curves and storing the information so he could later call upon the mental mold of her body for his art.

Although his arms were now wrapped around her, the more Mark tried to draw her closer to him, the less sensation he felt. The carnal urge to feel the pressure of her up against him was not being satisfied, and frustration began to set in.

"I want you." Was said hoarsely into her ear after he pulled his lips away from hers.

"I know."

Tightening his hold even more, he was almost to a point where he could not feel her anymore. A desperate "I'm losing you" came from him.

"Mark, you were never going to have me this way in the first place. I *am* only oil. You must seek out the real woman if you want to make love to me." The woman broke the embrace and without announcing her intentions, moved back two steps. "Is it love, Mark? Is this what you are experiencing?"

"I don't know." He whispered as he tried to catch his breath. "Do you need love to be a part of me?"

"Everyone needs love, Mark, but this is only a dream."

"No!" The desire within cried out. "Make it real!"

The look on her face told Mark that she was sharing the same emotions as he, but that it was impossible for them to advance past this point. Mark shut his eyelids tight against the reality of the situation, but the truth would not deceive him and he finally had to give into it.

"You're leaving now, aren't you?" Intuitively he knew this was what was going to happen.

The woman nodded her head and looked out to the water.

"Will you come back to me?" Mark asked as her hand delicately ran down his arm before she was out of his reach.

"No."

The woman began to walk toward the ocean and he didn't follow. Slowly she entered the still water and with every step she took deeper into the abyss, the more the element reacted to her presence. When she had reached the level of waist height, tides began to form around her, spreading out to cover the whole body of water.

The colors used to paint her began to separate as the oil swirled about her. The white from her gown and cream of her skin floated to the top, soon joined by the hue of her hair. Each individual color then blended together until it slowly dissipated into a film too thin to recognize.

Mark moved to the waters edge and sat down. Placing his right hand into the sea, he let the water lap over him while he rested his head on his knees. Mark's eyes never left the woman as she made her descent.

"Find me…" was called out to him before she disappeared into the tide. The woman's last step was taken too quickly and she missed the response he gave of "I will."

Mark woke up with a start. Wearily he sat up, the moonlight streaming in through his window illuminating his studio in a soft ghostly air that fit the afterglow of his dream. He looked around and saw nothing but his own apartment.

Getting up from the mattress that he used as a bed, Mark walked over to his drafting table and turned on the light he had over it. Sorting through the clutter, he found an old sketch pad and a pencil, clearing the work surface so he could place the tablet flat.

Then from memory, Mark Olson sketched the woman from the painting.

The End for now...

This short story was taken from *Dawn's Texas Love Stories* series. For more short stories and information about the author, please visit her on the web at *www.dawnroberts.net*.

~~..~~

Printed in the United States
77001LV00002B/25

9 781424 171309